"At least he has the opportunity to be raised by another mother who loves him..."

Zeke was speaking about her. Tears filled Kellyanne's eyes and she blinked them away. "I—I can't."

He reached for her hand and gripped it. "Kelly, you would be a wonderful mother to Brady. It's obvious how much you care for him."

She did. She'd loved this little boy since the first moment she'd seen him.

He pulled his hand away and stood and stretched. "Why don't I go find us some coffee or hit up the vending machine?"

She couldn't have endured all this without Zeke by her side but allowing him to get this close was dangerous to her heart.

The door opened again and, at first, she thought Zeke must have forgotten something. She wiped her face, needing to pull herself together. But when she looked up, she caught only a glimpse of a man's face beside her chair before he slammed something into her.

She fell off the chair and hit the floor, pain ripping through her head.

Her vision blurred but she fought losing consciousness... just long enough to see the man grab the baby and rush from the hospital room.

Virginia Vaughan is a born-and-raised Mississippi girl. She is blessed to come from a large Southern family, and her fondest memories include listening to stories recounted around the dinner table. She was a lover of books from a young age, devouring tales of romance, danger and love. She soon started writing them herself. You can connect with Virginia through her website, virginiavaughanonline.com, or through the publisher.

Books by Virginia Vaughan

Love Inspired Suspense

Cowboy Lawmen

Texas Twin Abduction
Texas Holiday Hideout
Texas Target Standoff
Texas Baby Cover-Up

Covert Operatives

Cold Case Cover-Up
Deadly Christmas Duty
Risky Return
Killer Insight

Rangers Under Fire

Yuletide Abduction
Reunion Mission
Ranch Refuge
Mistletoe Reunion Threat
Mission Undercover
Mission: Memory Recall

TEXAS BABY COVER-UP

VIRGINIA VAUGHAN

LOVE INSPIRED SUSPENSE
INSPIRATIONAL ROMANCE

LOVE INSPIRED® SUSPENSE
INSPIRATIONAL ROMANCE

ISBN-13: 978-1-335-72249-2

Texas Baby Cover-Up

Recycling programs for this product may not exist in your area.

Love Inspired
22 Adelaide St. West, 40th Floor
Toronto, Ontario M5H 4E3, Canada
www.Harlequin.com

Printed in U.S.A.

And I will restore to you the years that the locust hath eaten, the cankerworm, and the caterpiller, and the palmerworm, my great army which I sent among you.
—*Joel* 2:25

To Sami. Thanks for being a great writing partner
and a wonderful friend.

ONE

Kellyanne Avery pulled into her parking space at the apartment complex, disappointed to see her friend's car missing from its spot. She frowned. Lisa wasn't answering her phone, which wasn't like her, and she'd failed to pick up her four-month-old son, Brady, from day care. They'd had Kellyanne's number on file for emergencies, but this was the first time they'd had to use it.

Kellyanne glanced up at the window to Lisa's apartment where a light shone. She had to be home. But where was her car, and why hadn't she picked up Brady? Kellyanne had just gotten out of the car and opened the back door to retrieve Brady from his car seat when she spotted movement in the darkness and the outline of a man approaching her. Instead of unbuckling Brady, she reached inside her purse for the can of pepper spray she kept there. She was a single woman living alone in Austin, Texas, plus her job as a social worker meant she often went into the worst areas of town. With a father and five brothers in law enforcement, she knew how to protect herself, but that didn't stop her pulse from pounding in her ears as she backed out of the car. As he grew nearer, she raised the can and spun around to face him.

"Whoa, Kellyanne, it's me. It's Zeke."

As the man stepped into the light, she spotted the familiar handsome features of her old flame, Zeke Tyler. She almost hadn't recognized him without his cowboy hat, but she could never forget that Texas drawl. He'd filled out since the last time she'd seen him, but the kindness in his easy smile and the gentleness of his soft green eyes remained, even as they widened in surprise.

Zeke Tyler, the man she'd loved since high school.

Relief flooded her, and she lowered the can of pepper spray, trying to slow down her racing heart. "Zeke, you scared me half to death. What are you doing here?"

"I'm sorry. I didn't mean to frighten you. I knocked on your door and no one answered, then I saw you pull up. I promise I wasn't lurking around."

No, Zeke wasn't one to lurk about. She hadn't noticed him because she'd been concerned about her friend. "It's not your fault. I wasn't paying attention like I should have."

And deputy sheriff Zeke Tyler belonged to her hometown of Courtland, not to her life here in Austin.

She leaned into the back seat, unbuckled Brady and settled him on her hip before closing the car door. Zeke's eyes widened with surprise and then his brows furrowed. She saw his mind doing mental calculations. Those calculations would come surprisingly close to Brady's age, but she didn't want him to go there or ask her the question she saw on his face.

"This is my friend's son. She didn't pick him up from day care, so they called me. I'm the only other person authorized to get him." The last time she'd seen Zeke, during a visit to her family's Texas ranch, her on-again, off-again relationship with him had taken a turn, and she'd wound up pregnant. She'd lost the baby before she'd even had an opportunity to tell him. He had no idea he'd been a father for four precious months.

"Oh." Relief flooded his expression, but he looked like he was ready to bolt.

There hadn't been a good time to tell him about the pregnancy and miscarriage. At first, she'd been so devastated by the loss that she couldn't even comprehend telling him. She hadn't been back home since then and had decided this was something she needed to tell him face-to-face. Now was as good a time as any. "Why don't I take him to his mother and then we can talk."

He nodded and followed her up to Lisa's apartment across the breezeway from her own place. She'd met Lisa when she'd moved to this complex a year ago, and they'd become fast friends. Kellyanne had grown especially attached to four-month-old Brady, and it didn't take a genius to figure out why. He was close to the same age her own child would have been had he lived.

She raised her hand to knock but noticed the door wasn't fully closed, and the wood on the doorjamb splintered. Zeke noticed it too, and he pushed her aside, drawing his gun from a holster under his jacket before elbowing open the door and stepping inside.

Kellyanne moved behind him. The apartment was eerily quiet, but the place had been ransacked. Drawers stood open and their contents were scattered on the floor. Brady's toys were strewn and even the TV had been pulled down from the wall and thrown to the floor.

Zeke checked down the hallway and returned. He slid his weapon back into its holster and shook his head. "No sign of anyone."

She glanced around at the chaos and clutched Brady tightly. Who had done this and why? And more important, where was Lisa? "I don't like this."

Brady began fussing in her arms. She pulled his stuffed bear from the diaper bag and gave it to him. When she did, she spotted something protruding from behind the couch. She took a few steps closer and gasped. It was a foot.

She neared the couch, and her stomach dropped to her feet at what she saw.

Her friend was lying unmoving in a pool of blood, a gunshot wound to her head.

Zeke moved past her to the body on the floor. The woman was obviously dead, but he made a show of checking for a pulse anyway, since this was Kellyanne's friend. The body was cool to the touch, indicating she'd been dead awhile.

He stood and pushed Kellyanne toward the door. "We need to be careful not to contaminate the scene."

She clutched the baby against her, but let Zeke move her back outside into the breezeway. He pulled the door closed as best he could, took out his cell phone and called 9-1-1. "We need the police. A woman has been murdered." He rattled off the address and ended the call.

"Murdered? You think she was murdered?" Kellyanne's face went colorless, but her bright, blue eyes stared up at him. Must be the shock that made her ask that question.

"It looks that way. There's no gun." The absence of a weapon close to the body ruled out suicide. He'd seen his share of violence during his time as a deputy sheriff. More than he cared to admit. The police would come and have questions for Kellyanne. But first, she looked like she might be sick. He took the baby from her, and she leaned her arms against her knees, trying to catch her breath. She needed to sit down before she fell and also calm down if she was going to be able to answer the police's questions. He had a few of his own too. There were bruises on Kellyanne's face and arms. They were crystal clear in the sharp glow of the overhead light.

Someone had put those bruises there, and now her friend was dead. What had she gotten herself into?

"Why don't we wait for the police in your apartment," he suggested, and she nodded. They moved down the breezeway before she took out her key to unlock the door. Her hand was shaking, so he took it from her and opened it.

Zeke entered her apartment and spotted a portable crib pushed back into a corner. "Is this for him?" he asked, motioning to the child in his arms.

She nodded. "I babysit for Lisa sometimes."

He placed the baby into the crib and turned back to Kellyanne. Her entire body was trembling with shock and fear. He pulled her into a hug, soaking in the familiar feel of her petite frame against his body. He stroked her dark hair and she didn't pull away. After a moment, she buried her face into his chest and sobbed.

"I can't believe this. Who would do this?"

He had no answers to give her. Murders were rare in their small hometown but not unheard of. He'd had firsthand experience with that particular crime at a young age, having witnessed his father murdering his mother while he hid in the pantry. The slots on the door had given him a front-row view of the brutality and his father's suicide minutes later. He did his best to be dispassionate, yet every dead woman he saw took him right back to that terrible day.

But Kelly needed him, and that brought him back to the present. "I'm sure the police will do their best to find out. What can you tell me about your friend?"

She pushed away tears as she leaned against the counter. "We met when I moved here last year. We became best friends. She was a paralegal at a law firm downtown."

"What about her husband?"

"She wasn't married."

"The baby's father?"

She turned to glance at Brady. "I don't know who he is. She wouldn't talk about him. I sensed it was some big secret. He was probably married. But she loved Brady very much."

"I'm sure she did."

Sirens outside announced the local police's arrival. Zeke told her to stay inside while he walked out to meet the police and show them the scene. He watched as they cordoned off an area and called in a detective. When one arrived, he examined the body then asked to speak to the ones who'd found her.

Zeke showed his sheriff's deputy badge and introduced himself.

"Courtland County. What are you doing in Austin?" the detective named Shaw asked him.

"A buddy and I are in town for the Law Enforcement Expo."

He nodded. "I know some guys that are attending that. How did you know the victim?"

"I didn't. I know her neighbor Kellyanne Avery. We grew up together in Courtland."

"Okay. Take me through what happened and then I want to talk to her."

There wasn't much for Zeke to tell, but he explained about approaching Kellyanne and walking with her to her friend's apartment and finding the body.

"Any chance she already knew the victim was dead?"

He shook his head and bit back an angry retort. He knew Kellyanne. This detective didn't, and he had a job to do. "Her shock was real. She's still shaken by seeing her friend dead."

She was scared, and she had every right to be. A woman, her best friend, had been murdered only a door down from her. If this was random, it was terrifying to think about how close she'd come to being a victim.

The detective took down Zeke's information and headed inside to ask Kellyanne many of the same questions. Zeke followed him into her apartment but stood back as he sat at the table. Since Zeke had already spoken to him, it wouldn't matter much if he listened in, and Detective Shaw didn't ask him to leave.

Instead, Detective Shaw stunned him by recognizing Kellyanne "I know you. Don't you work for DFCS? We've had to call you in a few times."

He shouldn't be surprised that they had at least a passing recognition of one another. He knew Kellyanne worked for the Department of Family and Children Services, and social workers often came into contact with police officers.

Shaw continued. "You responded last month to the Finley case, where the parents were killed during a home invasion, didn't you? You came by and picked up the kids."

She nodded. "Yes, I remember you, Detective." She reached out and shook his hand. "It's nice to see you again."

"Too bad it's under these circumstances." He eased back in the chair opposite her. "What happened to those kids?"

"Their maternal aunt has taken custody of them. They're going to be all right."

"I'm glad to hear that. I understand you were friends with the victim across the breezeway?"

Kellyanne nodded and reached for a tissue as her eyelids moistened. "Yes. Her name is Lisa Adams. We met when I moved in last year." She motioned toward the portable crib. "This is her son. The day care called me when she didn't pick him up this evening."

Detective Shaw smiled at Brady and then asked Kellyanne to walk him through what had happened. Zeke listened as she went over the same events he had. He liked that the detective was being thorough.

"And how did you get those?" Shaw asked, pointing at the bruises on her face and arms.

Kellyanne's hand went instinctively to the dark spots on her skin. Zeke knew what they were. He'd seen bruising like that before. Someone had grabbed her and dug his fingers in, probably as he was dishing out the mark on her cheek. He wanted to step in front of her and stop the detective's questions, but he also wanted the answers too. If Kellyanne was involved in whatever had gotten her friend murdered, they needed to know about it.

"Lisa and I attended a fundraiser last night for Congressman Richardson. I was trying to find her to tell her I was ready to leave when I saw her arguing with a man. They were getting loud, and he grabbed her arm. When I tried to intervene, he grabbed me, too, and shoved me into the wall." She touched the bruise on her cheek. "That's where I got this."

Zeke's jaw tensed at the image of someone putting his hands on Kelly, but he kept silent and let the detective continue with his questioning.

"And who was this man?"

"I didn't know him, although it was obvious Lisa did. We didn't stick around to make introductions. She hurried to help me and we left."

"Did she tell you what the argument was about?"

"Not at first. She tried to insist it was nothing, but I could tell she was shaken. She finally told me it had something to do with

Brady's father." She picked at her fingernails, a habit Zeke knew meant she was nervous. She had good reason to be.

"Brady is her son?" When she nodded, he continued. "And who is his father?"

"I don't know. She never told me. It was some big secret. I assumed he was married, but I overheard her tell this guy she was arguing with that she had proof, and that she was going to expose him."

"Expose him for what?"

"I don't know. That's when I interrupted them and he pushed me."

Zeke walked out. He didn't want to know any more. It was almost a blessing she couldn't identify the man who'd shoved her, because he wasn't sure he could have stopped himself from marching over there and hammering the guy, given the opportunity.

He pulled out his cell phone and called Greg Frasier. They'd driven to Austin together to attend the LEO conference, and Greg would want to know where he was. They'd made plans to have dinner together at the hotel's restaurant, but Zeke was going to have to cancel. He needed to make sure Kellyanne was going to be okay before he even thought about leaving her.

His next call was to his boss, Josh Avery, the sheriff of Courtland County and Kellyanne's big brother. He would want to know about this.

"Is Kellyanne okay?" he demanded once Zeke explained the situation.

"She seems fine. She's shaken up, but she's okay."

Josh gave a loud sigh of relief. "I don't like this. I don't like knowing she's there alone. I'm glad you're there now." He paused and then asked the question Zeke had been dreading. "Why are you there?"

He'd always known her family had no idea about the real nature of their relationship. They'd been on-again, off-again for years, reconnecting whenever she flew back into town, which had become less and less frequent over the years. He'd done his best to convince her to stay, told her he wanted to marry her and would follow her anywhere if only she would let him. But Kellyanne Avery was a woman who wanted her freedom. The youngest of six kids and the only girl, she'd been stifled by her brothers growing up and was determined not to allow them to take over her life. She'd moved away from Courtland County right out of high school and made a life for herself alone in Austin.

And left Zeke behind.

"Never mind," Josh said before he could come up with an answer. "I'm just glad you're there."

"Don't worry about it. I'll make sure she's okay before I leave."

"And tell her to call me after she's done with the police, okay?"

"Will do."

He ended the call with Josh and walked back into the apartment where the detective was ending his questioning. "I'm certain I'll need to ask you some more questions." He glanced at the baby. "Should I call and make a request for someone to come and get him?"

"No need for that," Kellyanne insisted. "I'll make the report and take care of it myself."

The detective nodded. "Thanks for your help. I'm sure I'll have some more questions for you both, but for now, my condolences on the loss of your friend. We'll do our best to find out who did this." He handed them both a card with his name and number on it. "Call me if you think of anything else," he said as he walked out.

Zeke closed the door so she didn't have to

listen to the police working the scene down the hall. She didn't need that constant reminder that her friend was dead, murdered in her own home.

He glanced at Brady, who peeked at him through the mesh, and his mind shot back to his initial reaction at seeing him. He'd thought Brady belonged to Kellyanne and that implication had hit him in the gut. So much had changed since the last time they'd been together. He'd spent years pining after this woman, but he finally felt ready to move on. He'd gone back to church and recommitted his life to Jesus, but his past choices still carried consequences he was dealing with. He was thankful this little guy wasn't one of those consequences. But a pang of regret struck him, because he did want children. He'd hoped to build a family with Kellyanne, but she'd shut him down on marriage and family years ago.

She pulled a bottle from the diaper bag, picked up Brady and settled him into her lap. She looked natural with a child in her arms, but he would never tell her that since he knew her feelings on the matter.

"I spoke to Josh. He wants you to call him."

She shot him an angry expression. "Why did you call him?"

"For one thing, he's my boss. I needed to explain why I wasn't at the seminar he sent me to. Plus, he's your brother. He would paint my barn good if he found out about this and realized I hadn't told him."

She settled Brady back into his bed and turned to Zeke. "I don't need my brothers following my every move, Zeke. That's why I left Courtland in the first place."

He knew she hated that, and he couldn't blame her. With older brothers that included a sheriff, a former deputy, a US marshal, a former navy SEAL, and an FBI agent, their watching over her wasn't just the overprotectiveness of older brothers.

"This isn't just something you can shake off, Kelly. They have a reason to worry."

"And a reason to try to convince me to return to Courtland, where they can rule my life. That's not going to happen."

"They don't want to rule your life. They're just worried about you." He knew she loved her family, but she'd always been eager to get out from under their watchful eyes.

"I don't need a babysitter."

He stopped and took a deep breath. At least

he could tell Josh he'd tried. And speaking of babies. He glanced at Brady. "What's going to happen to him?"

"The state will try to find his father or Lisa's next of kin. If no one can be found, he'll go into foster care."

While he knew there were some kind and caring foster-care families out there, he'd also heard the horror stories. "I hope that doesn't have to happen."

A tear slid from her eye. "Me too." He could see she cared for the child and wanted to do what was best for him and her friend.

He put his arm around her. "You'll find him a good home. I know you will."

She turned to him and seemed to notice him for the first time. "Don't get me wrong, Zeke. I'm glad you were here today, but…"

"But why am I here?" It was a logical question. He'd shown up out of the blue with one mission—to finally put his feelings for her to rest. He reached into his pocket for the necklace she'd lost at the lake the last time they were together. The clasp had broken, and she'd been devastated to lose it since it had belonged to her grandmother. He'd found it after she'd left. He'd meant to fix the clasp and return it to her next time she came to town, but that had been a year ago. She seemed to have forgotten all about the necklace…and about him.

She gasped when he held it out to her. "My grandma's necklace. You found it."

"The clasp broke." He didn't tell her about the hours he'd spent out searching around the lake for it after she'd left. He'd convinced himself she wouldn't be gone long. He would hear from her soon, but as always, his calls and texts had gone unanswered.

She grasped the necklace and leaned into him, planting a kiss on his cheek. She'd probably meant it as a gesture of thanks, but he longed to pull her into his arms and kiss her full on the lips.

"You're welcome," he said and stepped away from her. "I should get back to the conference center. There's an evening class starting in an hour."

Her expression said she didn't want him to go, but he was already in too deep. He'd come for closure, not to get more involved, although he was glad he'd been with her when she'd found her friend.

"Well, how long are you in town?"

"Four days."

"Can I see you again while you're here?"

Everything inside of him was screaming to say no, but his heart wouldn't cooperate. He didn't want to be reminded of all the times she'd ripped it out and stomped on it. He just wanted to be with her. "You have my number, Kelly." The ball was in her court.

He opened the door but turned back one more time before he left. "Make sure you lock this door up tight. And call your brother."

He waited until he heard the locks turn before he left and walked past the police that were still gathering evidence from the brutal murder of Kellyanne's neighbor and friend.

He knew he wouldn't sleep tonight. And he knew he couldn't leave town when her life could be in danger.

Kellyanne pushed the grocery cart through the store to the baby aisle. She'd strapped Brady into the carrier in front of the buggy. The police had classified Lisa's apartment as a crime scene and wouldn't even allow her to gather any necessities for Brady, which meant Kellyanne had been forced into a grocery run. She had a few items in the diaper bag but not enough to make it through the night, much less the next few days. Except for the secondhand portable crib Kellyanne had, Lisa had always brought whatever Brady needed when Kellyanne watched him. Now he needed diapers, formula and baby food, and Kellyanne's apartment was woefully unprepared for a child.

Her cell phone rang, and she glanced at the screen. It was Zeke checking up on her. She wanted to take the call, but seeing him had felt too good. She didn't want to lead him on again when she knew there would never be a future for them together. Not when he found out her secret. Not when he learned the truth.

And when are you going to tell him?

She choked back hot tears. Now was not the time to focus on that. She needed to complete her shopping, get back to the apartment and put Brady down for the night. She needed rest too. This day had worn on her.

She pulled down a package of diapers, stunned at how much they cost. She would know the price of a child's needs if she'd been more careful, if she'd taken better care of herself while she was pregnant. She grabbed a few cans of formula and put them in the cart. She could wash and reuse the bottles Brady had in his diaper bag she'd gotten from the day care. She was grateful Lisa had paid ahead on Brady's tuition, since her bank account wouldn't cover day care costs too.

She knew she could place him in foster care. She did that every day with other people's kids, but she wasn't ready to do that with Brady, the sweet little boy with dark hair and blue eyes that always held a smile. They reminded her of Zeke's eyes in that way, even though his were green. She bit her lip and tried to focus on what she was doing.

She reached for several boxes of infant cereal and was about to place them in the cart when something jammed into her back, pressing her hard against the cart. Hot breath hissed on her neck. "Do what I say, and no one gets hurt."

Her throat went dry as fear rushed through her. "Who—who are you? What do you want?"

She tried to turn, but the man rammed what she suspected was a gun harder against her back.

"Don't look at me. Just take the baby and go. We're leaving."

She glanced at Brady in the buggy. He'd already lost his mother. If she went with this man, he would probably lose her too. She couldn't do that to him. Couldn't let that happen. She hesitated too long, and the man dug his fingers into her arm, causing her to cry out.

"We're walking out of here. Take the baby from the buggy now."

Her hands shook as she dropped the baby food into the cart and unlocked the strap keeping Brady from falling out. She lifted him into her arms and glanced around. Two people were in the aisle, a man at one end and a woman on the other. Both were preoccupied with their selections. She could cry out, but the man might shoot her or Brady. But what would he do to them if she left with him?

Nothing good.

She stepped backward and accidentally bumped the shelf of baby food, sending a display tumbling, jars busting at the man's feet. He swore and jumped back, his attention diverted. She took advantage of the distraction and screamed for help and ran to the front of the store, tripping over her own clumsy feet and falling to the floor. Brady fell, too, and started crying, but at least she hadn't fallen on top of him. A crowd quickly gathered around her.

A man reached to help her to her feet. "Are you okay, ma'am?"

"Someone's after me. He has a gun." She pointed toward the baby aisle and the man helping her turned and scanned the area before raising his hand.

"There he is! Get him!" She looked up to see her attacker running for the front doors and vanishing as two strangers chased after him.

A woman picked up Brady and tried to soothe him before handing him back to Kellyanne. "I don't think he's hurt. He just got scared."

She clutched the baby. He wasn't the only one. Remembering the man's hot breath on her neck sent shivers down her. How had he tracked her here, and what would have happened to her if she hadn't gotten away?

The manager rushed over and led her into his office. "Why don't you have a seat? I'll phone the police. You'll be safe in here."

"Thank you."

He handed her a bottle of water. She placed Brady on the cushions of the seat and opened the water. It felt good against her parched throat. He hung up the phone. "The police are on their way. Don't you worry. He can't get to you in here. You're safe. I need to go check the floor, but I can remain with you until the police come if you'd like."

She shook her head. "No, thank you. You've done enough. We'll be fine."

He headed for the door. "Feel free to lock this behind me if it makes you feel better."

It did. She stood and locked the door and then walked back to the couch. Brady was calming down, but he was hungry and needed a change, and the diaper bag was in the car. She would have to deal with that, but for now, all she could do was relive the horror of that man pushing a gun into her back. She took out her phone and hovered her fingers over the last number that had called her. Zeke. She shouldn't call him. It wasn't his concern, but she wanted his comfort and the familiar, safe feeling of his arms around her.

She put the phone away. She'd made her choice. She wouldn't put him through this again. He deserved peace, and she was nothing but chaos and bad decisions. She slid the phone back into her pocket and turned to Brady. It was time to learn to take care of herself.

Zeke was in an evening class focused on new technologies available to law enforcement when his cell phone buzzed in his pocket. He glanced at the screen and saw the number for the local police department. Probably more questions about Kellyanne's friend that he couldn't answer. His gut clenched, realizing how little he knew about Kelly these days.

He motioned to Greg that he would be right back and then slipped from the room to take the call. "Tyler."

"Deputy Tyler. This is Detective Shaw of the Austin PD."

"I remember you, Detective. What can I do for you?"

"I just received word that your friend Kellyanne Avery was involved in a failed kidnapping attempt at a local grocery store."

His heart fell into his stomach, and the air left his lungs. "What? When? Is she okay?"

"Both she and the baby are fine. Someone tried to abduct them right in the baby aisle at the Food Mart. She managed to run for help, and a couple of Good Samaritans chased the guy from the store."

"So he got away?"

"He did, but I'm told the store has video of the incident, so we have a possible good lead."

He was grateful she and Brady hadn't been

hurt or taken, but why was Detective Shaw phoning him? Why hadn't *she* phoned him?

"I'm heading down to the store. I thought you might want to join me there?"

"Is it still an active scene?"

"It is. My officers tell me the lady is pretty shaken up."

"Text me the directions. I'm on my way." He shot a text to his friend that he wouldn't be returning to the lecture hall and then pulled up the ride-sharing app on his phone. He and Greg had driven to town in Greg's car, but he'd already borrowed it earlier in the night and couldn't leave his friend without a ride back to the hotel.

By the time he made it to the grocery store, only two cop cars remained. He pushed his way to the front until he saw Detective Shaw. "How is she? What's happening?"

"She's fine and so is the baby. They're in the office. I've already taken her statement about what happened. Some guy she didn't recognize shoved a gun into her back and told her to grab the baby and walk out of the store. She knocked down a display and used the opportunity to get away from him." He took out his phone and pulled up a photograph of a man wearing a hat and a dark jacket. His face was largely hidden by the hat. "The store has a good surveillance system, so they were able to give us a photo of the man. Do you recognize him?"

He stared at the photo but no name came to him. "I don't. Did Kellyanne recognize him?"

"No. She claims she didn't get a good look at him."

"And no one caught up with him?"

"We're tracking down leads, but it looks like he got away clean."

He shook the detective's hand. "Thanks for calling me."

"You're welcome. I heard the call and recognized Miss Avery's name."

He didn't like thinking this attack had anything to do with Lisa's murder, but he couldn't help but make that connection. "How did he know she was here? And why try to grab her out in public instead of at her apartment where there would be fewer witnesses?"

Detective Shaw shrugged. "She was at her friend's apartment earlier trying to get some supplies for Brady. Maybe the killer was watching the police working there, saw her with the baby, and followed her here. He might not even know where she lives, but if she saw him arguing with the victim, he might want to find out what she knows about him."

"So you do believe this has something to do with Lisa's murder?"

He shrugged before walking away. "It sure would be coincidental if it didn't."

Zeke knew he was right. Coincidences happened, but where murder was involved, nothing was above suspicion.

"I'll have patrol cars driving by her building just to be safe."

He thanked Shaw and then walked into the manager's office and saw Kellyanne leaned back against the couch, the baby on her chest, and his heart swelled at the sight. What he wouldn't give for that to be his child. It was all he'd ever wanted with her, but it would never happen. His heart had been beaten and hammered too many times already.

He knelt beside her and called her name. Her eyelids fluttered open, and her blue eyes looked at him, full of surprise. "Zeke. You're here."

He nodded. "Detective Shaw called me." He wanted to ask why she hadn't called him but didn't. He might hear that she didn't want him around. "Are you okay?"

Tears welled in her eyes. "I was so scared."

"I know. You did good though. You got away from him."

He found it interesting that he'd specifically told her to take the baby. It was possible he just didn't want someone noticing the child had been left alone, but Lisa had told Kellyanne her argument had something to do with Brady's father, and now her friend was dead. Was he trying to get his hands on the child now that Lisa was dead? Or get to Kellyanne because she'd seen his face and could testify about the argument? Whichever it was, it took a lot of bravado to try to abduct someone from a busy shopping center. He should ask Detective Shaw to check the security footage outside. This man might have had an accomplice waiting in a vehicle for him.

"Let me drive you home."

She stood and picked up Brady. "I didn't get to finish shopping. I still need to get diapers and formula."

He walked with her through the store and gathered the things Brady needed. At the checkout, the cashier smiled at them and gushed at the baby. "What a beautiful family," she said as Zeke pulled out his credit card and swiped it.

He noticed the way Kellyanne blushed, but

neither of them corrected the woman. She must not have been working earlier during the attempted abduction. "Thank you," Zeke told her and carried the bags out to Kellyanne's car. "Why don't you let me drive?"

She handed over the keys and strapped Brady into his car seat. He scanned the area but didn't see any dark figures lurking around. No one was watching that he could see, but it was those he couldn't see that worried him.

She directed him to her apartment, and he made certain they weren't followed. They got out and moved quickly past the door to Lisa's apartment that now had crime-scene tape covering it. He unlocked her apartment door, and she carried Brady inside, placed him into the portable crib and then pulled out the items they'd purchased. She was shaken. He could see it in her demeanor and the way she chewed her lip.

He moved toward her and tilted her chin up to look at him. Unshed tears had made her lashes wet. He stroked her cheek. He'd meant to comfort her, but everything inside of him wanted to pull her into his arms and kiss her. He checked that. He couldn't think of her like that. In a few days, he would be gone, and she would be here. Alone. He didn't like that idea either. He wanted her back in Courtland. But then he'd always wanted her back in Courtland. His wanting it had never made it happen.

He helped her put the few groceries away and then ordered in supper, and they ate in silence. He didn't want to leave, but as the time grew later and later, he knew he had to.

"Are you going to be okay here alone?"

"I'll be fine," she assured him, the jut of her chin showing him her determination. Why did she push him away like that when he just wanted to help her?

"I'm only a phone call away."

She held on to his hand until he had to pull it away for her to close the door.

He stood there staring at her door as he heard her turn the locks and move away. He leaned against the wall beside it. She might not want him there, but he didn't feel right about leaving her. Her friend had been murdered, and now someone had tried to abduct her. Both events had shaken Kellyanne to her core. He would've slept in his car if he'd had one.

He placed his hand on her door and said a silent prayer for God to watch over Kellyanne and Brady tonight since he couldn't.

TWO

The next morning, Kellyanne awoke to discover four text messages and a voice mail from her brother Josh, reminding her that she hadn't phoned him and checking to make sure she was okay. She gritted her teeth as she replied that she was fine and that everything was under control. She hated that Zeke had called Josh, but she guessed she understood his position. If Josh had discovered what had happened and that Zeke hadn't told him, it could cost Zeke his job...or at least some goodwill with his boss. Yet, it didn't ease her mind to have Josh in the know about what was happening in her life.

And speaking of supervisors, Kellyanne phoned hers to let her know what had happened. She needed to take a few days off to recover from finding her friend dead and to decide what to do about Brady. She doubted her boss, Dana, would have a problem with her keeping Brady with her temporarily since she was listed as Lisa's emergency contact at the day care but, eventually, she would have to come up with a long-term plan for him.

She was right about Dana's reaction. "Take all the time you need," she told Kellyanne after learning about her friend's death. "We'll cover your work. And don't worry about Brady. He's better off with you at the moment than in emergency foster care."

Kellyanne thanked her for understanding and ended the call.

As she did, another text from Josh popped up. Glad you are ok. Keep me updated.

She sighed and crawled out of bed, hating the idea that Josh expected her to report to him. He might be sheriff of Courtland County, but she was a long way from home. On the other hand, if she didn't do as he asked, he might spill what had happened to the rest of the family. Her parents, along with three more of her brothers—Josh, Paul and Lawson—were in Courtland, but it was her other two brothers that could show up unexpectedly at her door. Miles's secret work with the marshals service could have him anywhere in the country, while Colby traveled often with his work as an FBI agent.

No, it would be better to placate Josh until he realized there was nothing to worry about.

With work and family squared away, Kellyanne turned her attention to Brady, changing, feeding and dressing him before loading him into the car and heading for the day care. Since she wasn't going in to work, she could keep Brady with her, but she wanted to keep him on as much of a regular schedule as she could. So far, he'd been fine, but he was at the age now that he could recognize people, as evidenced by the big smile he always gave her when he saw her. He had to miss his mother and wonder where she was and when she was coming to take him home, even if he couldn't ask the question. A pang of sadness filled Kellyanne when she thought that Brady would never have any real memory of Lisa. Her friend deserved to be remembered.

She dropped Brady off at the day care and spent several minutes with Patrice Elliot and Alice Jenison, the two women who owned the day care, as they expressed their grief over Lisa's death.

"We saw it on the news last night," Alice

said, her eyes brimming with unshed tears. "It's just awful. She was here only yesterday."

"Do they know who killed her?" Patrice asked, but Kellyanne had no answers for her.

"They've just started their investigation. It'll take some time."

Patrice watched as Brady tried to roll over on a mat in the infant room. "What about him? What will happen to him?"

"I'll keep him until we can find a good home for him."

"We'll help any way we can," Alice assured her.

"That's right. Lisa was paid up through the end of the month, but we can work something out if need be."

"Thank you both. I appreciate it. I want to keep him on a regular schedule for now. I think it will help him. But I also need to keep him safe. I want to make sure you both understand that I'm the only person who should be picking him up."

They glanced at one another before nodding in agreement. Alice responded. "Of course. You were the only other person beside Lisa on the pickup list and we never release a child to anyone not on the list."

"Are you expecting any trouble?" Patrice asked.

"No, of course not. I'm just trying to be thorough."

They must have seen the concern on her face because they went through the security measures they had in place. She already knew about the secure entrance where visitors had to be buzzed in, but Patrice showed her the security cameras and alarms, as well. Kellyanne left feeling better about Brady being there.

She wiped away tears as she returned to her car. Lisa had had so many people that cared about her and Brady. But if last night had taught her anything, it was that there was someone out there who didn't share that sentiment. She kept hearing Lisa's comment that the confrontation with that man at the fundraiser had something to do with Brady's father. Had he been at the fundraiser? Was he the one who'd fought with Lisa and shoved Kellyanne…was he the one who murdered Lisa?

Her phone buzzed with a text message. She glanced at the screen and smiled. Zeke.

Good morning. I'm at your house and I brought coffee.

She smiled and texted him that she'd gone to the day care and would be home shortly. It was thoughtful of him to bring her breakfast. Truthfully, if Brady hadn't awoken and needed tending to, she might have just slept in all day. Her head was aching from worrying about what had happened to her friend and the attack on her, all the while shouldering the responsibility of finding a home for Brady when she couldn't imagine parting with the little guy.

Zeke was at her door when she arrived back at her apartment. He smelled freshly showered and shaved, and she liked the look of him in the morning. She'd forgotten how handsome he was, but she shook away those memories of him. She was just feeling vulnerable.

"And here I was worried I would be getting you out of bed," he admitted as he walked in behind her and set the cups of coffee and food bag on the table next to her kitchen.

"Lisa usually has Brady at the day care by seven a.m. She was always an earlier riser, so he was up early too. I thought I would try to keep him on as normal a schedule as possible."

"That's a good idea." He handed her a cup,

and she opened the top and soaked up the aroma of coffee. She fell into a chair as he handed her a breakfast sandwich and then pulled out the chair opposite hers and settled in it. She was suddenly very aware of how she looked. She'd put on jeans and tennis shoes and pulled her hair up into a bun for the quick drive to the day care. Not exactly the glamorous look she would have liked for him to see, but the past twenty-four hours had done a number on her. So much so that crawling back into bed and sleeping all day didn't sound like a terrible idea.

"Thank you for this," she said, biting into the sausage and biscuit.

"I confess, I have an ulterior motive. I wanted to make sure you were all right."

She shrugged. "I didn't sleep well, and Brady was up early. All I kept thinking about was Lisa lying in that apartment all alone. I wonder how long she was there before…"

He turned the conversation away from their grisly discovery. "Were you home at all yesterday? Did you see or hear anything?"

"No. I worked all day. I was on my way home when I received the call from the day care that Brady hadn't been picked up."

"And you didn't talk to your friend all day?"

He was asking questions as a cop would. What had she seen? What had she heard? Was she certain she hadn't spotted the guy? Irritation bristled through her. "Any more questions, Deputy? Would you like a pen and paper to jot down some notes?"

He leaned back in his seat, a frustrated sigh leaving his lips. "This isn't for an investigation, Kelly. I'm concerned. Someone was murdered in the apartment across the hall."

"I know that. Trust me, I know. I didn't see or hear anything. I didn't even know anything was wrong until the day care called me."

"Okay."

She turned to face him. "Are these Josh's questions?"

"No." He stood and folded his arms across his chest. "They're mine. I'm worried about you. Is that so wrong?"

"It's not your business to worry about me."

His expression drooped and she felt shame rush through her. She hadn't meant that as harshly as it had sounded. The truth was she was glad he was here, but she didn't want him here as a cop. She wanted him here as a friend.

Her face warmed. She'd lost the ability to call him a friend or anything else the day she left town, and she'd ruined any chance they might ever have at a future when she'd lost their baby before she could tell him about it.

She'd been waiting for the right time to tell him about the miscarriage. This wasn't it, but it was as good a time as ever. After all, she might never see him again once he returned to Courtland. Or worse, the next time she saw him, he might be married with kids of his own. It was time he knew the truth.

"Zeke—"

Her phone rang, interrupting her confession. She picked it up and glanced at the screen, worrying when she noticed the number to the day care.

"Kellyanne!" Patrice's voice was filled with worry, and it immediately sent Kellyanne's heart racing.

"Patrice, is something wrong? Is it Brady? Is he okay?" Images of him falling and hitting his head or suddenly becoming ill rushed through her. She'd been looking after him for one day, and he was already in trouble.

"Everything is okay. Brady is safe. But there is a man here who wants to take him. He claims he's Brady's father. He isn't on the approved list of names, so we don't want to let him in. I know we just talked about it this morning, but I wanted to check with you to see if you knew him?"

Panic rose in her. Who was this man? "I don't know him."

She heard a commotion on the other end, and Patrice call out to Alice.

"Patrice, what's happening?" Kellyanne asked.

"He's gone now. He got mad and raced off when Alice refused to let him through the door."

"I'm on my way."

Zeke was two steps ahead of her. He grabbed her keys and opened the front door for her. She rushed to her car and slid into the passenger's seat.

She gave Zeke directions, and a few minutes later, they pulled into the day care's parking lot. They both jumped from the car, and Patrice buzzed them inside.

"Are you both all right?" Kellyanne asked. Alice was on the floor with an ice pack on her forehead while Patrice hovered over her.

"We're fine," Alice insisted. "He tried to push his way inside, but I managed to close the window before he could get through, but then I slipped and hit my head on the desk."

The day care had an interior locked door to

the facility to prevent intruders. There was a window to the sign-in desk that the man had obviously tried to get through.

They both looked at Zeke. "Who is this?" Patrice asked.

"This is my friend Zeke." Kellyanne rushed through to the back room where Brady was still safely in his walker, oblivious to what had happened. She heaved a sigh of relief and was even more relieved when Zeke wrapped his arm around her shoulder.

"He's okay."

She returned to the front office and questioned Patrice and Alice. "Tell me about this man."

"He seemed perfectly normal. He said he was Brady's father, and he wanted to pick him up since Lisa had died. When we told him we couldn't let him go without proof, he grew angry."

"Did you ask to see his license or ID?" Zeke asked. She could kiss him. Always the cop.

"He didn't want to give it. He just kept saying it was his right to have his child. I told him if he didn't leave, I would call the police. To be honest, I have no idea who Brady's father is. Lisa never listed his father on her admission forms, and only Kellyanne is listed as someone who can pick up Brady."

"You did the right thing," Zeke assured her. "Did he at least give a name?"

"Yes, Jim Durban." She looked at Kellyanne. "Was that man Brady's father?"

"I don't know. I never met him, and Lisa never told me his name. I've never heard the name Jim Durban."

"What about your security cameras?" Zeke asked. "Do you have him on video?"

Alice hurried to the computer and pulled up the video feed. The man who'd tried to take Brady looked perfectly normal. He had dark hair that was similar to Brady's, but she didn't recognize him. He wasn't the man Lisa had argued with at the fundraiser, or the man who'd attacked her at the store last night.

"Can you print that?" Zeke asked, and Alice obliged him. He handed the photo to Kellyanne. "Maybe one of her other friends knows who he is."

"Should we call the police?" Patrice asked. "He did try to push his away inside, but if he really is Brady's father..."

Kellyanne shrugged. "If he comes back, give him my number. He can call me. If he can prove he is who he says he is, we'll make arrangements through the agency. He'll have to go through the courts to get legal custody. In the meantime, I think I'll take Brady home with me just to be safe."

They agreed that was a good idea, and Kellyanne retrieved Brady and his things. She didn't know if this man was who he claimed to be, and that was a problem. If he was Brady's father, where had he been for the past four months? And why had Lisa never talked about him? Whoever he was, if he showed up again, he was going to have to prove his paternity. And then he would have plenty of explaining to do about his part in possibly murdering her best friend.

She loaded Brady into his car seat, and Zeke drove them back to the apartment. She could see his mind was working, trying to figure everything out, and she was once again glad he was here with her. She needed to do some digging to see if she could locate Brady's birth certificate. If it listed Jim Durban as the father, she would go from there.

They returned to her apartment, and Zeke placed Brady into the crib. He was an active baby, already pulling up onto his elbows from his tummy and reaching for things. She needed to get his toys from Lisa's apartment or purchase new ones. He needed to be able to get down and play and roll and pull up, and she worried about her lack of baby supplies stunting his growth. Once again, she realized how unprepared she was to look after a child.

Zeke seemed to read her mind with his next question. "What are you going to do if this guy shows up again?"

"I won't just hand Brady over to a stranger. I need some kind of proof of who the father is. Maybe I can track down his birth certificate. Do you think the police will let me search Lisa's apartment for it?" She had no idea where Lisa had kept her important documents, but it was a place to start.

"Doubtful. Besides, if there were any legal papers like that, the police probably seized them. I need to update Detective Shaw about what happened at the day care and pass along the name Jim Durban and the photo Patrice gave us. I can ask him then about getting some stuff from Lisa's apartment."

Before she could agree to him making that request, another thought occurred to her.

"I just remembered Lisa brought a box of things and stored it in my closet a few months ago when they were replacing her floors. She didn't want the contents ruined, and she never returned for it."

She jumped up, went to her bedroom and opened her closet door. Zeke followed her, and when she pointed to a box on the top shelf, he easily reached for it and pulled it down. He placed it on the bed, and she opened the top. It was a box of papers. "Looks like her important documents. No wonder she didn't want them ruined." She found an envelope marked "Birth Certificates" and opened it. She pulled out a folded sheet of paper with the name Brady Michael Adams listed at the top. Hope rang through her that they would finally know if the mystery man from the day care was indeed Brady's father. She scrolled down the page, but it was blank where the father's name should be listed.

She handed it to Zeke and fell onto the bed. "There's no father listed."

He glanced at it and then returned it to the box. The excitement they'd both felt moments ago faded. "And you have no idea who she was seeing when she became pregnant?"

"I didn't even know her then. We met when I moved in here, and she was already several months pregnant by then."

He pulled out another envelope, opened it

and scanned it. "You should see this, Kelly." He handed her the papers. It was a legal document with the words "Last Will and Testament" in bold letters at the top. Kellyanne felt the sorrow of her friend's death hit her again. "She had a will."

"Look who it names as Brady's guardian in the event of her death."

She scrolled down the page and was shocked to see her own name along with instructions on what to do in the case of her untimely death. "She wants me to take Brady."

"She trusted you."

"I guess she did." But how could she be expected to look after Brady when she hadn't been able to take care of her own baby?

She put her hands over her face as sorrow swept over her. She and Lisa hadn't known each other long, but they'd become good friends, and Lisa had taken on the role of a protective older sister, the sister Kellyanne had never had growing up. Having Lisa look out for her was somehow different from having five older brothers always in her business. She hadn't minded Lisa's overprotectiveness. Lisa had always said she'd made enough mistakes in life and didn't want Kellyanne to have to repeat them.

"I'm sorry about your friend," Zeke said, kneeling beside her. "You've had all of this thrust at you, and you haven't even had time to grieve for her."

"She was a good person, and she loved that baby so much, Zeke. She wanted so much for him."

"We'll figure this out."

She touched his face and wanted to fall into his arms. "We? Does that mean you'll stay with me?"

"I'm not going anywhere until I know you're not in danger. Your brother would hog-tie me and cook me over a fire if I let anything happen to you. I should call and update him."

She grabbed his arm. "Don't you dare. This isn't any of his business."

He knelt beside her again. "Kellyanne, he's your brother and my boss. I have to tell him."

She'd run as far from Courtland County as she could get to get away from the prying eyes of her family. Having five older brothers and being the only girl and the baby of the family meant she had everyone watching her every move. She'd endured their overbearingness more times than she cared for. This wasn't Josh's jurisdiction, and it wasn't his business. "He doesn't need to know."

"I'm only in town for a few days, and I haven't even gone to most of the seminars I signed up for. He'll want to know why I wasn't there. What should I tell him?"

"I don't know, Zeke, but I need you here, and I need you to protect my privacy."

"He'll just call the local cops and speak to Detective Shaw."

"It's not his business." She got up and walked to her dresser, hanging her head as the tears threatened to come again. She didn't want her business broadcast to the rest of the family and have to endure questions and lectures about moving away and living on her own. She didn't want their opinions. She wanted everyone to stop treating her like a child and let her live her life. In fact, given that Josh knew about Lisa's murder, she was surprised that none of her brothers were already knocking on her door and demanding she return home.

Zeke stood behind her and gripped her shoulders. "If you really don't want me to tell him, I won't. It'll be our secret."

She turned and stepped into his embrace, burying her head against his chest and basking in the feel of him as he tightened his arms around her. She soaked in the musky scent of his cologne, cologne she'd bought for him years ago, and she was thankful to know he still used the same scent. It reminded her of simpler days when the only things she had to hide from her brothers were her meetups with Zeke. They'd run off the first boy she'd ever brought home, interrogating him relentlessly until he'd decided being with her wasn't worth being on their bad sides. She knew they hadn't threatened him or been mean, but she also knew how intimidating they could be. From that day forward, she'd determined to never give them that opportunity again. She'd never brought home another boyfriend for the family to grill. Not even Zeke.

Especially not Zeke.

If only Zeke had come with her when she'd left town. They might have had that family she'd dreamed about having with him. But his life was in Courtland, and his grandmother had been ill. He wouldn't have left her, so Kellyanne hadn't even bothered asking. He'd never been able to leave Courtland County, no matter how badly the town and life had treated him. She'd thought he would want a fresh start, but he was stuck in a town that would forever see them both as kids.

She heard fussing from down the hall, breaking whatever spell there was between them. Brady needed her. She pushed away tears and stepped out of Zeke's embrace. She didn't have time for sorrow or grief or even self-pity. She had a child to think about, and even though it wasn't the one she longed for, she loved Brady and would do her best for him. And she would keep him safe even if it was the last thing she ever did.

Zeke returned to his conference for afternoon classes, assuring Kelly he would be back to check on her later that day. She was fine with that. She had no plans except to try to get some rest. Her head was still aching, and she felt worn down by the events of the past twenty-four hours. The possibility that Brady's dad could show up and walk off with him, combined with the uncertainty of knowing he might have taken part in Lisa's murder and her attempted abduction weighed heavily on her mind. Was this Jim Durban really Brady's father? She needed more information on this man, information only the police could verify.

She picked up her cell phone and dialed Detective Shaw's number. When he answered, she explained about the man who'd gone to the day care to try to get Brady.

"I know. Your friend Deputy Tyler already informed me. I wish you or the day care had called me when it happened."

"The man gave his name as Jim Durban. I found Brady's birth certificate in a box Lisa left in my closet, but there's no father listed. Is there any chance you can check this guy out for me?"

He gave her a low chuckle. "Aren't I the one supposed to be doing the investigating?"

"I'm not investigating. I just want to know what to do in case he shows up again."

"You don't let him near you or the kid without a court order. Besides, if he shows up, Brady's paternity may be the least of your worries. It's possible this guy was involved in the attack against you and in your friend's murder. Text me the photo. I'll check him out."

"Thank you, Detective Shaw."

She sent the text and put away her phone, but she still couldn't rest. Her mind was spinning with the details of everything that had happened. She was right that this man might be responsible for the attack against her. She pressed her hand against her head and wished she could remember more, wished she'd pressed Lisa more about the argument she'd had with the man at the fundraiser. She'd heard Lisa tell him she had evidence and that she was going to expose him. But what evidence did she have, and what was she going to expose? And had it gotten her killed?

She needed visual stimulation. She typed in the congressman's fundraiser and immediately found photographs of the event, and even a few from the after-party. She glanced at the faces of those in the photographs. No one seemed familiar. No one stood out.

She grabbed Brady and headed out. She needed to try to jump-start her memory. Maybe if she was there, back in the conference room, something might spark a memory. It was a long shot, but at this point, it was all she had. Figuring out who Lisa argued with during that party might help her discover who killed her friend.

She pulled into the parking structure for the West Hills Hotel and Conference Center, took out the stroller and strapped Brady in before heading toward the entrance. She found the conference room where the event had taken place. The tables were once again set for an event, and the white dishes and glassware gave her a familiar feeling. The plush carpet beneath her feet sparked a memory she couldn't quite grab hold of, but she thought she recalled laughter and music. She glanced up and remembered there had been brightly colored balloons on the ceiling.

Detective Shaw would get around to questioning everyone who was there, but Kellyanne didn't want to wait on police procedure. She knew all too well the investigative process could be tedious.

"What are you doing here?"

She turned to see a woman dressed in heels and business attire. Her hair was upswept, and she held a clipboard.

"Who are you?" Kellyanne asked.

She smirked. "I was going to ask you the same thing."

"My name is Kellyanne Avery." She reached out her hand. "I was here the night before last with Lisa Adams."

The woman's harsh expression softened, and she smiled and shook Kellyanne's hand. "I heard about Lisa on the news. I'm so sorry. Do they know what happened to her?"

"Not yet." She shuddered, recalling seeing her friend's blank expression and lifeless form. "But it looks like someone shot her."

She gasped and pulled her hand back. "You saw her?"

"I found her. Someone attacked her inside her apartment."

The woman's hand fluttered to her necklace. She looked like she was going to break down, but she quickly regained her composure. "My name is Casey Morgan. Lisa and I both volunteered on Senator Davenport's campaign a few years ago. I'm an event planner, and they still call me whenever they need something. I made the arrangements for the fundraiser the other night. I'm here now prepping a different event."

Kellyanne didn't know any of Lisa's co-workers or friends. Lisa had seemed to cut them off, choosing to spend all her time with Brady or with Kellyanne. "Were you and Lisa close friends?"

"We were for a while."

"Then you know who Brady's father is?"

"Who is Brady?"

She felt her heart fall. So they weren't such good friends. She motioned toward the stroller. "Brady is Lisa's son. I'm trying to figure out who his father is now that's she's gone." She reached into her purse and produced one of her business cards with her name, occupation and phone number. "I'm a social worker with DFCS."

Casey took the card and nodded, but tears smudged her mascara. "I didn't even know she'd had a baby. We hadn't seen one another in a while. She quit the campaign and seemed to drop off the face of the earth. I never knew why."

"When was that?"

"About a year ago." She looked at Kellyanne and seemed to recompose herself. "However, that doesn't explain why you're here. I'm setting up for another event. You shouldn't be here."

"I came here because I'm worried that something that happened here got my friend killed."

Casey paled again. "What are you talking about?"

"I found Lisa arguing with a man. They were both very angry. Now she's dead. I'm concerned he might have had a hand in her death. I'd like a list of the names of everyone who attended the party."

"I can't give that to you. It's privileged information."

"I'm sure the police will want that list too." They may even already have it. She was pushing it, and she knew it. The last thing this woman wanted to do was talk about what happened at that party or who might be involved. Kellyanne could see the worry on her face.

She gave Kellyanne a hard stare. "Then the police can request it. You were a guest at that party, and the accusations you're making are deplorable. I refuse to listen to another slanderous word. You need to leave now." She spun on her heel and walked out without another word.

Kellyanne pulled out her phone and texted Casey Morgan's name for Detective Shaw to check out. She seemed to know more than she was letting on.

Kellyanne put away her phone and sighed. She hadn't accomplished what she'd hoped, but she was more certain than ever that Lisa had been right in her decision to cut these people from her life.

During a break in sessions, Zeke texted Kellyanne to check in. His friend and fellow deputy, Greg Frasier, sat down beside him and shook his head.

"You texting her again?"

"I'm just checking in?"

"Man, this woman's got you wrapped around her little finger."

He slid his phone back into his pocket, his face warming at his friend's accusation. "She does not."

"From the moment we arrived in town, she's had you at her beck and call."

"She's in danger. Her friend was murdered and someone is after her. If something happens to her, Josh will have my hide."

"Does he know why you went to see her in the first place?" Greg was one of the few people who knew about his past relationship with Josh's sister.

Zeke shook his head. "No, he doesn't, and I would appreciate it if you didn't tell him."

"It's none of my business. I'm just here for the seminars and the free meals. And for a few days without the kids screaming in my ear every five minutes."

Zeke smiled. Greg had three little kids all under five at home and a wife he adored. Zeke enjoyed spending time over there playing with the kids and seeing the way Greg and his wife, Carla, acted around one another. He could recognize two people in love, and they were.

He had to admit that he was jealous of Greg. He had the life Zeke had always wanted. He was living the dream, while Zeke was still sitting on the sidelines.

He took out his phone again and glanced at the screen. How many days had he spent waiting for Kelly's call or text message? Too many. And he'd always ended up disappointed.

He should have stuck the necklace in the mail and been done with it, but he couldn't be sorry he'd come. Not when her life was in danger. Maybe he could never be the man she loved or wanted to be with, but he could keep her safe. Safe for the man who would one day take his place. It wasn't right, and it wasn't fair, but it was all he had. He couldn't leave her, knowing she was in danger. He wouldn't want to, even if his feelings for her weren't a part of the equation.

The announcer called everyone back inside. Zeke stood and checked his phone one more time for a message from Kelly. Nothing.

Greg shook his head and chuckled as

he headed for the conference room doors. "Wrapped around her little finger."

Zeke put away his phone.

If her little finger was all he could have, he would take it.

Kellyanne buckled Brady into his car seat and headed home. She was still mulling over what Casey Morgan had had to say and trying to force herself to recall what had happened. One thing she knew for certain, she didn't want to be alone tonight. She hoped Zeke would come over again.

She pushed away that thought. She was getting too close to him. Too dependent on him. He was going to be leaving soon, and she would be on her own with Brady. It was daunting to think about taking care of him on her own, but she would do it. A tear slipped down her face. She missed her friend, and Brady missed his mom. This entire episode had her thinking about family and wishing she were closer to them to ask for advice and to seek comfort. She loved them, but their need to treat her like a little girl irritated her to the point she'd gotten as far away from them as possible after high school.

She wished Zeke were going to be in town

longer, but nothing would pull him away from Courtland for long. She had to tell him about the pregnancy and miscarriage before he left town. She couldn't keep this secret from him any longer, couldn't let him leave town without knowing about the baby. She used her hands-free to dial his number and a soft shudder of delight filled her when his gentle baritone voice answered.

"I was wondering if you'd like to come to supper at my place tonight. I'll cook for you. There's something we need to talk about."

"I'd love that, Kelly."

"Good. I'll see you in a few hours, then?"

She ended the call and glanced in the rearview mirror at Brady. Nervousness tickled her insides. Tonight, she would come clean about everything. She would tell him about getting pregnant and the miscarriage, and she expected that would be the end of their time together. It would be over between them once he knew the truth.

She stopped at the grocery store, cautious as she purchased items for homemade lasagna. She breathed a sigh of relief when they made it through their shopping without incident. She hated the way her mind was now always on alert, always looking out for the next attack. Would her life ever get back to normal? She loaded the groceries and Brady into the car and headed for her apartment.

She was on the interstate when an SUV approached her quickly from behind. She changed lanes to give him plenty of leeway to go around her. The traffic wasn't heavy, and he had plenty of room, but she'd learned there were some crazy drivers in this town.

The car changed lanes, too, coming up beside her. She glanced over and saw the window coming down and the barrel of a gun sticking out. She jammed the steering wheel as a shot fired. The window behind her shattered. Brady screamed and so did she, but she pressed her foot against the accelerator and took off. The car quickly caught up, and a man leaned out to take another shot.

Kellyanne made a sharp turn and plowed down an exit ramp. The car kept on, unable to turn in time. It did slam on its brakes, and she heard the squealing of tires as it tried to stop. She didn't stick around to see what happened and made a left on the off-ramp, thankful for the lack of traffic and green light. She headed down a path, turning again and again with no sense of direction or idea about where she was going, except that she knew she had to get away from the men with the guns.

Brady was crying in the back seat, the shattered glass and gunfire no doubt having terrified him. At least, she hoped he was only frightened and not injured. She needed to stop and check on him, but first, she had to make certain they were out of danger.

She zoomed through a shopping center parking lot, turned into an alley that led to the back of the center and stopped the car. Her hands were shaking, and her heart was pounding. Her pulse pounded like a jackhammer in her head. She had no idea who those men were or why they'd opened fire on her.

She stopped, watching and listening intently for any evidence that they'd somehow caught up with her. But how could they? She'd made so many turns even she didn't know where she was.

She stared out the window, scanning the area. No one was in sight. She heaved a sigh of relief. Brady continued crying, but it was more like a whimper now than a terrified wail. She turned to check him for injuries. He seemed unharmed by the bullets or shattered glass, so she spoke a few comforting words to him, hoping to calm them both.

She jumped when her cell phone rang, her heart hammering in her chest again until she realized it was Zeke calling. She hit the answer button, but all she could get out through a choked voice when she answered was his name. "Zeke."

Panic rose in his tone in response to her shaky voice and possibly the baby crying in the background. "Kelly, what is it? What's wrong?"

"Some men. I was—I was driving home, and they shot at me."

"Someone shot at you? Where?"

"On the interstate. They shot out my passenger window. I managed to get away. I'm hiding behind a shopping center, but I don't know if they're still out there. I don't know if they'll find me again."

"I'm on my way. Tell me where you are."

She glanced around but realized she was in unfamiliar territory. "I don't know. I don't recognize anything."

"All right, Kelly. Listen to me. Use your GPS on your phone. Tell me where you are."

She kept her foot on the brake as she pulled the phone from the cradle and keyed up her GPS. Her hands were shaking so badly that she nearly couldn't make the app open or type in her home address.

"Okay, I've got it."

"Where are you?"

"Ten miles from my apartment."

"Kelly, start driving. Park at the shopping center around the corner from your apartment complex. I'll meet you there. I don't want you going home alone."

"And you'll stay on the line with me?"

"Yes, darling. I will most definitely stay on the line with you the entire time."

She set the phone back into the cradle before inching her car from behind the shopping center. She scanned the area but didn't see the SUV. She pressed the accelerator and sped toward the interstate ramp heading back to her apartment, but her eyes were constantly scanning her surroundings, watching in the rearview mirror. Zeke's voice on the line was a welcome distraction from her fear. By the time they reached the turnoff to the shopping center, Brady had fallen asleep.

She pulled the car into the lot and spotted Zeke leaning against his car. He ended the call when he saw her. She pulled to a stop in front of him. Her hands shook as she opened the door, unbuckled her seat belt and walked toward him. He reached for her hands first and then pulled her to him. She clung to him, pressing her face against his chest as tears flowed. She couldn't do this alone. She couldn't do this without him.

THREE

He hugged her to him, and she allowed it. He hated to see her so upset, but she hadn't even had time to process what had happened to her friend. Zeke waited with her as the police arrived and she answered their questions about the attack then they left her car to be processed and he drove her back to her apartment in Greg's vehicle. He watched the baby as she cried herself to sleep in the other room. He longed for nothing more than to go to her and comfort her, but that wasn't his place any longer.

Funny, he'd come to Austin with one agenda aside from the conference—to end things between them once and for all. Instead, he was more wrapped up in her life than ever. She drew him to her like she had her own gravitational pull on him. He was powerless to resist. He longed to be with her and be a part of her life.

He put away the food they hadn't cooked and washed the dishes. As he stared out the window above her sink and out into the dark sky, he wanted to scream. Why was this happening to her, and what could he do to make it all go away?

God, please help me help her.

Even his prayer felt impotent. He had no control when he was around her, no control of his life or his will. She drew him in, and there was nothing he could do or say to make this better for her.

He pulled out his cell phone and called Josh.

"How's my sister?" He was always right to the point.

"I'm worried about her."

He explained the situation and imagined Josh's face as he listened, twisted and just as angry and helpless as he felt.

He heard something hit the wall through the phone and knew Josh had thrown it. The frustration was evident in his voice when he spoke. "Why does she have to be so stubborn?"

He didn't have an answer, so he kept silent instead.

"Technically, I can't order you to look after her."

"You don't need to."

"I don't suppose there's any chance you can convince her to come home?"

He blew out his breath. It was all he wanted. "She hasn't been receptive to the idea."

"Do your best, and keep me updated. I haven't told the family about this. They don't need to worry. That's my job."

It was Zeke's job, but Josh didn't know that. He ended the call and slipped the phone back into his pocket. He wandered into the living room and glanced around at the simple furnishings that included several photographs of him and Kellyanne goofing around. Happier days. But it made him feel good to know that she'd kept them.

He knelt and watched Brady sleeping peacefully in the portable crib, and his mind once again went to what might have been if Kelly hadn't left him. They might have been married by now and had a couple of kids of their own. Too young, some would say, but he'd always felt older than his years, and no one could deny his love for her. She'd captured his heart years ago. But loving her had kept him in a circling pattern, never being able to move on with his life or land on something solid. For years, every time she'd come into town, she'd sent his heart into a tailspin with her words of love for him, but then she would leave again.

Why, Kelly? Why wasn't I ever enough for you?

He saw the necklace he'd returned sitting in a dish on her coffee table. It had been his sole excuse for coming to see her. To end it. He was glad he hadn't mailed it. No matter their past, she needed him now, and he was going to be here for her. But he couldn't let his heart go down this road with her only to be shattered again.

He had to protect himself.

I'll help her, God. I'll be here for her, but please help me guard my heart.

The next morning Kellyanne awoke early. Brady was still asleep in his bed and Zeke was sleeping stretched out on her couch, his long legs hanging over the end. She hated to see him so uncomfortable but was glad he'd chosen to remain. She wouldn't have been at ease staying here alone after being shot at. The shooting could have been a random crime that had nothing to do with Lisa's death, but as she stared at Brady in the crib, she couldn't get it out of her head that someone was out to get her.

Was it the mysterious man who'd assaulted her? Lisa's ex? Brady's father?

She'd spent hours last night trying to recall something, anything that might lead them to the mysterious man who'd shoved her at the fundraiser. He had to be involved in these attacks against her. If he wasn't, he certainly knew who was.

She left both Zeke and Brady sleeping and jumped in the shower. When she came back out of the bedroom, Zeke had given Brady a bottle, started the coffeepot and fixed eggs and toast for breakfast. The smell of bacon frying reminded her of home, and she smiled.

She enjoyed having him around.

"How are you feeling this morning?"

She felt her face flush. "Foolish. I shouldn't lay all of this on you. This isn't your problem."

He looked stung by her words and turned away, and she wanted to kick herself. That wasn't what she'd meant.

"I only meant that you have a job in Courtland. You're in town for a police convention. You aren't here to coddle me."

He leaned against the counter and locked eyes with her. "Taking care of you isn't coddling. You're in danger and under a lot of strain. I'm glad I'm here."

"I'll bet your friend is wondering where you were last night."

"Naw, I texted him to let him know I'd meet up with him this morning."

"I need to take Brady to the day care and go to the office. But first, I need to arrange for a rental car."

"I'll drop you by the rental agency."

"Is it on your way?" she asked. He smiled and licked bacon grease from his finger. "It can be. But are you sure you want to take him back to the day care? What if that man returns?"

"I can ask Mrs. Reynolds across the hall. She watches him sometimes for Lisa." She'd been watching him the night of the party. Mrs. Reynolds was a widow with one son she rarely saw who lived on the East Coast. She kept the toddlers at church and longed for the pitter-patter of grandchildren one day, although her son didn't appear to be in any hurry in that department. She'd been happy to offer her babysitting services whenever Lisa needed them.

"That sounds like a good idea."

She phoned Mrs. Reynolds, who assured her she was available today to watch Brady. "It's so sad what happened to Lisa," she told Kellyanne. "It just breaks my heart."

"Mine too," Kellyanne said.

The older woman eyed Zeke when Kellyanne carried Brady across the breezeway. "He's an old friend from my hometown," Kellyanne explained. "He was with me when we found Lisa."

"He's very handsome," she noted and then turned her attention to Brady, who laughed and giggled when she made a funny face at him.

"Have the police questioned you yet?" Kellyanne asked her. Her apartment shared a wall with Lisa's. If anyone had heard anything that day, it would be Mrs. Reynolds.

"Yes, they asked their questions, but I didn't know anything. I didn't hear any commotion over there. I was out most of that day. It must have happened while I was gone."

Kellyanne thanked her again for watching Brady and promised to be back in a few hours. "I'm not going to work. I just have a few things I want to take care of at the office."

"Take your time. Brady and I will be just fine."

Zeke drove her to the rental agency and pulled up to the front before sliding the car into Park. He didn't get out, and she didn't move to get out either. She knew this might be the last time she saw him before he returned to Courtland. She didn't want to acknowledge that, and there were so many things she wanted to say to him, things she needed to tell him, but the time had never seemed right.

They were never right.

"When do you leave for home?" she finally asked, breaking the silence between them.

"Tomorrow's the final day of the conference. Greg and I will head back afterward."

"So you're free tonight, then?"

He looked at her and smiled. "I am."

"Can we try supper at my place again? There's something I need to talk to you about." It was time he knew the truth. That for a few brief months, he'd been a father.

He nodded. "I'd like that."

She got out and went inside. Zeke waited until they pulled a car around for her then he transferred the car seat into it. He opened the driver's door for Kelly and she slid inside.

"I'll see you later tonight," he said before telling her goodbye and getting back into his car. She felt the lack of his presence as he drove away.

She arrived at her office only to have her coworkers huddle around her to express their worry and condolences.

"What happens to the baby?" one of them asked.

Lisa's will stated that she wanted Kelly-anne to raise him, but she couldn't take that risk, not after she'd failed with her own baby. "I'll have to find a good home for him."

"You don't have to do that alone, Kelly-anne. We can help."

She knew her coworkers would do their best, but she wasn't ready to part with Brady yet. He was her last connection to her friend, and she wasn't ready to put him into the system. There were plenty of people who would want to give him a home, so finding one wouldn't be difficult.

"I left Brady at my neighbor's, but I wanted to get a few things from my desk, if that's okay." She looked at Dana, who nodded.

"Of course."

The group dispersed, but Dana followed Kellyanne to her office. "I talked with Human Resources. Technically, taking guardianship of this child entitles you to up to six weeks of family leave, the same amount of time as if you'd given birth or adopted a child."

Kellyanne was grateful to have a boss who looked out for her employees. "Thank you, Dana. I might need to use some of that."

She nodded. "Then I'll start the paperwork."

Kellyanne settled into her desk and turned her attention to the task she'd come for. Brady's birth certificate might not have provided the father's name, but Lisa had to have family somewhere that needed to be contacted, and Kellyanne hoped to use the agency's systems to locate one of them. She needed to locate Lisa's next of kin to determine the proper place for Brady to be. Lisa might have expected Kellyanne to keep Brady, but she wasn't qualified to be a mother, not when she hadn't been able to even care for her own child. Brady would be better off with a different family and a mother who knew how to care for him.

She glanced at the phone on her desk and saw the voice mail light flashing. She pressed the button and listened, jotting down notes to give to Dana to handle while she was out.

The third voice message stopped her cold.

"Hi, Kelly, it's me." Kellyanne's heart leaped into her throat. Lisa's voice. Lisa had always been bad about choosing her office number instead of her cell number from her contacts list. It had been a running joke between them. "I just did something stupid. I went to confront Brady's father. His staff wouldn't let me see him, but I made it known that I've got pictures and emails that prove the affair, that prove he's Brady's father. I was so stupid. I thought I was protecting him by staying away and remaining silent, but he used me, Kelly. Last night, at the party, I discovered he carried on with other women too." Her voice choked as she continued. "He never loved me. He used me. I'm going to expose him for who he truly is. He's a powerful man, Kelly, and this will destroy him. I'm afraid he's going to send someone after me. I'm scared. If something happens to me, take the flash drive to the police. Show it to them. I hid it in—" A loud crash sounded, and Kellyanne's heart plummeted as her friend screamed in terror. "No, don't! I don't—" A pop of gunfire sounded and the call ended.

All the air left her lungs as she sat stunned by the unexpected message from the dead. Had she just overheard Lisa being murdered?

She dug through her purse for Detective Shaw's card, quickly dialed the number and told him what she'd found.

"Can you play it for me?"

She didn't want to hear it again but hit the play button and listened again to her friend's final words, probably her final moments. It was just as horrific the second time around.

Shaw gave a loud sigh on the other end of the phone. "We're still going through the contents of her apartment, but I don't see a flash drive listed on the evidence log. Do you know anything about it?"

"No, I don't."

"We're in the process of pulling her phone records. We'll track down each number she called. We can go back to the time before Brady was born. There will surely be calls between them then. Plus, we're tracking her GPS and credit card info. We'll find out who is behind this."

"Thank you, Detective."

She ended the call with him, dropped her cell phone and put her head in her hands. Hearing Lisa's voice one final time had been a punch in the gut. She was trying so hard to be strong for Brady's sake, but this was just too much.

She picked up her phone to call Zeke, only to have it ring before she could. She hit the answer button. "Hello?"

She was met with silence for a moment before a whispered voice spoke. "I was at the party the other night. I saw what happened."

"Who is this?"

"My name isn't important. I know you've been looking for answers about the man Lisa argued with. I saw everything. I can give you the answers you're looking for."

Her heart leaped into her throat. "You saw the man Lisa argued with? What was his name?"

"I can't talk about it over the phone. Meet me in the Café Brew Coffee Shop now. No cops. I'll answer all your questions, but if I see a cop, I'm leaving."

Her pulse pounded as the line went dead. Was this finally the break she needed? Was she about to discover who killed Lisa? Who Brady's father was? And who was responsible for the attacks against her? She should call Detective Shaw and let him know about this meeting, but the caller had said not to involve the police. She grabbed her cell phone and shot off a text to Zeke with the information the caller had given her. He texted back right away that he was on his way and not to go without her. But he was more than twenty minutes away. She couldn't risk the caller leaving if she didn't get there quickly. And what would he do when he saw Zeke? He wasn't wearing his deputy's uniform, but he had cop written all over him. Hopefully, his presence wouldn't scare off this lead.

She waited as long as she could and then reached for her purse, put her phone on voice mail and walked out. She couldn't wait for Zeke any longer. Hopefully, he'd show up on time, but she couldn't risk this lead walking out if he didn't.

I'm going to find out who killed you, Lisa.
She raced down the hallway to the elevator and saw it was out of order. She pushed open the stairway door. It was faster to take the stairs anyway. Her office was on the sixth floor, so going down the stairs would be the easy part. Coming back up would be more difficult, but she wasn't planning on returning, at least not today. She still needed to try to find a relative of Lisa's, but this day had already drained her.

A figure moved above her, and she spotted someone hurrying from the floor above. She half turned just as he came up behind her and shoved her hard, sending her tumbling down the stairs. She reached for something to stop her fall, but her hands found nothing.

She hit the first concrete step, and pain ripped through her arm as she landed on it and then kept tumbling, slamming into each step as she fell. Pain stole her breath. She reached for the railing but wasn't able to grab hold. She knew she was screaming, but all she could hear was the slamming of the hard surface against her skin and a ringing in her ears as she hit the bottom step. Her head was spinning, but she saw a figure approaching and knew he wasn't there to help. She tried to move but could do nothing but cry out.

Suddenly, the door to the stairwell entrance slammed open and a figure turned and darted up the stairs. Someone knelt beside her and called her name.

Zeke!

Relief filled her even though his expression was full of concern. He hovered over her, his lips moving, but she couldn't make out what he was saying as the darkness pulled her under.

* * *

She was a mess, but she was fortunate no bones had been broken. She'd fallen hard down a flight of stairs. He'd gotten to her offices as fast as he could but had been surprised to find her lying hurt on the stairwell floor. The image of a man standing over her was burned into his memory. He'd had the choice of checking on her or running after him. He'd chosen Kellyanne.

The paramedics were insisting she go to the hospital, but she was awake now, alert and refusing to go. She'd only lost consciousness for a few minutes, but they had been the most gut-wrenching minutes of his life.

"Kellyanne, please go to the hospital. You need to get checked out."

"I'm fine," she insisted, but she didn't seem fine when she gasped in pain as an EMT placed an ice pack on her face. More bruises. She was beginning to look like she'd gone three rounds with a boxer, and he didn't like it one bit. "Besides, I can't leave Brady."

"Brady is fine. I'll go pick him up myself if I need to."

Her eyes widened suddenly. "The caller. The man at the café. Zeke, did you go there? Did you meet with him?"

"No, I came right here to pick you up. You were supposed to be waiting for me."

She fisted her hands. "He must think I didn't want to meet him."

"Or he used that call to lure you out and tried to push you down the stairs. Did you ever think of that? There might not be anyone with information. It might have all been a trap."

"But if it wasn't, I just lost my chance to find out the name of the man who killed Lisa."

He rubbed his face. She was always so stubborn. "How did he know how to reach you, Kelly? How did he know you were looking for answers?"

She pondered that question for a moment. "I told Casey Morgan that I worked for DFCS. I gave her one of my cards with my number on it and told her I was looking for the man Lisa argued with at the party. Maybe she spread the word. She made me believe she wouldn't, but she must have given the caller my information."

"I'll call the café. Maybe someone left a note. Or we'll see if Shaw can get the security tapes. We can figure out if someone was even there and try to track him down. The important thing is you're safe." He squeezed her hand because it seemed to be the only part of her body that wasn't injured. He couldn't resist her pleas to check on the man at the café, even though he was certain it had been a trap to lure her out. If it would make her feel better, he would check the café out, but he insisted she allow the paramedics to finish with her first. While they were waiting, Detective Shaw showed up, questioning what had happened.

"I heard your name over the radio and came by. Are you all right?"

She looked up at him. "I will be." She went through the events and Detective Shaw took notes.

"The man who pushed you. Did you recognize him? Was it the same man from the day care?"

Zeke answered that question. "It wasn't the man from the day care surveillance. He was wearing a hood, but it came off while he was running away. The man who pushed Kellyanne down the stairwell had blond hair. The guy from the surveillance had dark hair and looked older."

"This wasn't the man from the grocery store either, or the one I saw Lisa arguing with at the party. I didn't get a good look at the man who shot at me, but I don't think it was him."

"That means we're looking for more than one person. Whoever is behind your friend's murder has people working for him."

Kellyanne stared at him, her eyes wide with fright. "Lisa did say in her message that he was powerful."

"I don't care how powerful he thinks he is. He won't get away with this. I'll talk to security in the building to find out if they have any footage of this man. I'll also take care of calling the coffee shop."

"Thank you," Zeke said, shaking the man's hand.

Kellyanne's cell phone rang, and she dug through her purse for it. He was amazed that thing had survived this attack without being smashed to bits. She scrunched her face as she checked the caller ID. "It's Brady's day care."

Zeke was surprised they would be calling. "But you didn't take him there today."

"I didn't. I asked Mrs. Reynolds across the hall to watch him." She answered the call, and he heard a frantic voice respond.

He grabbed the phone and put it on speaker. "What happened?"

The voice that responded was choked and crying. "That man. He came back demanding for us to let him have Brady. I told him Brady wasn't here and tried to give him your number."

His gut clenched, and he sensed something bad was coming.

"He pulled a gun. He demanded to know where you lived, but I don't have your address."

"What did you tell him, Alice?" Kellyanne asked, her face full of fear.

She sobbed. "I'm so sorry, Kellyanne, but he threatened the kids."

"What did you tell him?"

"I didn't have your address, but I told him you live next door to Lisa."

Her eyes grew wide, and she stared up at him. "He's going after Brady."

Kellyanne pushed the paramedic away. "I have to get to him."

"We'll take my car," Detective Shaw stated, and she and Zeke followed him to his police cruiser. He used his radio to call to see if another cruiser was closer, but they were only minutes away.

They climbed inside and headed toward her apartment building. Worry riddled through her. Had he found her apartment? Had he taken Brady? She pulled out her phone to call Mrs. Reynolds to warn her that someone might be on their way to try to snatch Brady. The call went right to voice mail. That couldn't be good.

"What was the point of this?" Detective Shaw asked. "Were they trying to keep Kellyanne busy while they snatched the baby? Or did they target her to tie up loose ends?"

Zeke shook his head, but she saw worry on his face, as well. "I don't know, but Brady is obviously in danger."

She bit her lip to keep from crying out.

It only made sense that this was the doings of the mysterious father, the man Lisa had confronted at the fundraiser. Who was he? And what would he do with Brady if he got his hands on him?

They reached the apartment and rushed up the stairs. Zeke drew his gun and pulled her aside as he and Detective Shaw went up first. Mrs. Reynolds's door was standing open. She motioned to Zeke, who nodded that he saw it too. Suddenly, Kellyanne remembered Alice had told the intruder she lived next door to Lisa. Next door. Not across the hall.

Zeke pushed open Mrs. Reynolds's door and glanced inside. Detective Shaw followed him. As the men moved through the apartment, Kellyanne spotted Mrs. Reynolds sprawled across the kitchen floor.

"Whoever was here is gone," Shaw stated as he and Zeke returned and holstered their weapons.

Kellyanne hurried to Mrs. Reynolds. She was bleeding from a nasty gash to the head and was unconscious but alive.

"Brady." She hurried into the spare room where Mrs. Reynolds had a crib set up for the kids she periodically watched. Kellyanne burst into the room.

The bed was empty.

Brady was gone.

She screamed and fell apart. Zeke hurried behind her and held her up as tears flooded her. They'd taken him. They'd taken Brady.

She should have known she wasn't up for this. She wasn't mother material.

"We'll find him," Zeke promised. He held her shoulders, forcing her to face him. "We will find him. They won't get away with this."

But they had gotten away with it. They'd killed Lisa and taken her son. And she still had no idea where Lisa's mysterious flash drive was hidden. There was no proof of the affair.

Shaw appeared at the door. "The lady's waking up." He rushed back to the kitchen, and Zeke followed him. Kellyanne remained by the door to the spare room. Her legs wouldn't work. She couldn't move. Brady was gone and nothing else mattered.

She'd lost another child.

"I've called for an ambulance," Shaw stated. "Ma'am, are you okay? Do you know where you are?"

Mrs. Reynolds sat up, and with a little help from Zeke and Shaw, she made it into a chair. Her eyes were wide with shock, and she grimaced in pain. "A man… He pushed me inside…demanded to know where the baby was."

And she'd told him. She didn't want to blame Mrs. Reynolds. She wasn't in any condition to fend off an intruder, especially one that was armed, but a wave of anger rushed through her.

Kellyanne knew the truth. This was her fault. She'd been the one to leave Brady here unprotected while she went off pursing her answers. What did it matter who had attacked her as long as Brady was safe? It didn't matter. Not anymore.

"It's okay," Zeke said, his voice kind and tender. "You did what you could."

He pressed a towel from the counter against the gash on her head as she continued to try to form words to explain what had happened. "I had just put Brady down for a nap, but I realized I'd forgotten the diaper bag. He must have seen me with it."

"You were outside?" Kellyanne asked.

"Just in the breezeway. When I realized I'd forgotten the diaper bag, I wanted to return to my apartment to get it. That's when he saw me and pushed me back inside."

Kellyanne's heart hammered in her chest. She glanced at Zeke, who locked eyes with her. They were both asking the same question. "Mrs. Reynolds, where was Brady when this happened?"

She looked at Kellyanne, and the cloudiness seemed to fade from her eyes. "In your apartment. I knew you would be home soon, so when he started falling asleep, I carried him over there and placed him in his bed. I was going to sit with him until you got home. When the man demanded to know where he was, I told him he was gone, that you'd picked him up and left."

Kellyanne bolted from the apartment and across the hall. Alice had said she'd told the man Kelly lived next door to Lisa, not across the hall, so he must have thought Mrs. Reynolds's was the right place, especially once he saw the bag with Brady's name written on it and the crib in the spare room.

She threw open her front door and rushed inside, stopping when she spotted the tiny figure in the portable crib sleeping soundly, his gentle snoring tugging at her heartstrings. He'd had no clue what had taken place. She turned and fell right into Zeke's embrace as so much emotion struck her—relief, gratitude, love. She bent down and picked Brady up, and he fussed at being woken, but she didn't care. She needed to hold him in her arms to prove he was okay. He hadn't been taken. He was safe because of Mrs. Reynolds's quick thinking.

Zeke pulled them both into a hug, but one thing was certain. Both Kellyanne and Brady had been targeted today.

"Kelly, I hope this incident has convinced you that you need to take measures. You need to leave town, come back to Courtland with me," Zeke said.

Detective Shaw had made his report and processed the scene, and Mrs. Reynolds had been taken to the hospital for overnight observation. She'd given a good sketch of the man who'd attacked her, and with both her testimony and the daycare workers', the police would hopefully be able to identify and capture this man soon. Detective Shaw had confided to Zeke that the name the man had given at the day care was most likely an alias and that they hadn't yet been able to locate him or confirm his identity. Until they did, Kellyanne and Brady were still in his sights… and Kellyanne still had no idea where the flash drive they were after was hidden.

Zeke had to convince her to return with him.

She started to object, but he didn't let her finish.

"If not for you, then think about Brady. I don't know if they want him because he's proof of an affair, or if they just want to use him to force us to turn over the evidence we don't have. You have to keep him safe. After today, it's obvious that someone is targeting him. We can protect him better in Courtland than here. We'll have your family and your brothers and the entire sheriff's office on his side."

She turned and bit her lip. She was so against returning that it made him think she was going to be stubborn, but she needed to do this. She needed to get out of Austin. Returning to Courtland made the most sense. He'd seen the way she'd wilted when she'd thought she'd lost Brady. He never wanted to see her like that again. He would protect both of them no matter what.

"Listen to me. I know this is something you don't want to do, although I confess that I don't understand why. But we have to protect Brady. And I have to protect you. We have to think about him now, put his safety before your own needs and desires."

She turned to look at him, and guilt flooded her expression. Finally, she nodded. "You're right. I have to think about his safety first." She glanced at Brady and then back at Zeke. "I'll go pack."

He breathed a sigh of relief once she disappeared into the bedroom to pack her suitcase.

Finally. Now maybe he would be able to keep her safe.

FOUR

Kellyanne watched as the familiar landscape passed by. They'd left for Courtland
right away. Brady was in the car seat in the
back of her rental car while Zeke drove. As
much as she enjoyed being with Zeke, returning to Courtland was the last thing she'd
wanted. She missed her family and had lots
of good memories of growing up in Courtland
and the Silver Star Ranch, but those memories were often overshadowed by her family's
incessant prying into her life. They couldn't
seem to accept that she was a grown woman
with her own life, even now that she lived
hundreds of miles away. She needed the distance from them to keep her sanity, yet here
she was, jumping right from the frying pan
into the fire by asking for their help.

Zeke had been right to convince her to
come. She had Brady to think of now, which

meant she had to put aside her own wants. She was a mother now, at least for the time being. She had to put his needs and safety first. If she'd done that before with her baby, Zeke would be a father. She glanced over at him smiling and drumming his finger to a song on the radio, oblivious to the fact that he'd fathered a child he knew nothing about. Despite her previous desire to tell him, she couldn't do it now. She and Brady needed him.

She spotted the turnoff approaching that would take them to Silver Star, and she braced herself to face her family, but Zeke bypassed the turn and continued straight.

"Josh asked us to come by the sheriff's office before the ranch," he told her when she started to ask.

"You told him we were coming?" She shot him a glare, which he responded to with a shrug of his shoulder.

"What was I supposed to do, Kelly? He's still my boss. I had to tell him."

She crossed her arms to try to convey her displeasure, but she didn't blame him. Of course, he'd been in contact with Josh. He certainly owed her brother much more than he owed her. Josh had taken a chance on him and given him a job at the sheriff's office. All she'd done was left him again and again. Besides, it didn't matter if Josh found out about her return home in five minutes or a half hour from now.

They approached downtown Courtland, and Zeke parked the car in a spot on the street in front of the courthouse adjacent to the sheriff's office.

She spotted Josh approaching the car and got out to greet him, not even bothering to unbuckle Brady from his car seat since it looked like they weren't going inside to meet with him. She stared down her brother, ready to defend herself against what he probably thought was her putting herself in danger.

He shook Zeke's hand and then pulled Kellyanne into a hug before holding her shoulders at arm's length and studying her. Worry creased the lines around his eyes. "Are you okay? Really okay?"

His concern was genuine, and some of her irritation faded. "I'm really fine," she assured him. Despite his meddling, she knew he loved her.

"Zeke filled me in on what's been happening with you. I have to admit, I wish you'd called and told me."

"What could you do, Josh? It wasn't your problem."

He sighed and pulled a hand through his hair. "Anything that places my kid sister in danger is my problem, Kelly. Don't you forget it."

She bit back a retort, knowing her brother was only looking out for her, but she still wasn't going to agree everything in her life was Josh's business.

"Zeke, I appreciate all you've done for my sister, but this isn't your fight. My brothers and I will take over now. We'll keep Kelly and the baby safe while we figure out who is behind these attacks."

She stiffened as Zeke glanced back at her, and thought she spotted hesitation on his part. *Oh no, please don't leave me alone now, Zeke.*

Finally, he spoke. "I'd rather stick close by, if you don't mind, Josh. It doesn't feel right to walk away now."

Josh glanced between them as if he knew the history between them. But he couldn't. She'd been so careful, and she was certain Zeke wouldn't have told him. "If that's what you want, we'll take all the assistance we can get. In that case, why don't you drive Kelly-anne back to the Silver Star. I asked Lawson and Paul to meet me there after I finish up with a meeting I have scheduled. We need to talk about what's been going on and how to keep her safe."

"We'll see you then," Zeke stated before Josh turned and headed back toward his office. Zeke glanced at her from over the top of the car. "We should go."

Before they could get back into the car, someone called his name. They both turned, and Kellyanne spotted a petite woman approaching them and waving at Zeke.

"I thought that was you," she said. "Glad to see you're home. How was your convention?"

"Joanne, hi." Zeke glanced at Kellyanne and then back at the woman, and Kellyanne thought she saw sweat beading on his forehead.

Who was this woman who garnered such a reaction?

"I just arrived back in town."

She shot Kellyanne a curious look and then glanced at the baby in the car. A frown formed on her face. "Looks like you had an interesting trip." The friendly tone she tried so hard to convey didn't quite reach her face, and Kellyanne noticed curiosity there.

Zeke's face reddened. "Joanne, this is Kellyanne Avery. We drove back from Austin together."

She reached out her hand to shake it. "Yes, I've heard of you. Nice to meet you."

"You too," Kellyanne responded, noticing the way her eyes tracked to the baby through the car's window.

"And who is this?"

"His name is Brady," Kellyanne told her. "He's my son." She glanced at Zeke and made a snap decision. "Actually, he's *our* son."

Zeke's eyes widened in surprise. She hadn't meant to blindside him with that revelation, but she suddenly realized they needed to keep Brady's identity a secret in case someone came to town looking for the child of a murdered woman.

The shock on Joanne's face nearly matched Zeke's. She turned to face him before somewhat composing herself. "Well, congratulations to you both. When did this happen?"

Zeke pulled a hand nervously through his hair. "I just found out myself." It wasn't a lie, and Kellyanne couldn't help the smirk that formed on her face.

"I guess your trip was more eventful than you'd planned, wasn't it?" Joanne turned to hurry away, but then she looked back at Zeke.

"We can talk later. I'll see you at church on Sunday?"

He nodded and waved to her. Once she was out of earshot, he spun to face Kellyanne. "Why did you tell her that?"

Her amusement at the situation faded at the serious tone of his voice. "I don't know. I just suddenly realized we needed to keep Brady's identity a secret. What if someone comes looking for him?"

"You should have talked to me before you said that," he insisted, climbing into the car.

She got in too. "You're right, and I'm sorry, but we have to do whatever it takes to keep him safe, don't we? I don't know if it'll do much good if the bad guys know who I am, but it couldn't hurt, could it?" She saw he was struggling with this and was hurt at the implication. "It's not so far-fetched that he could be our child, is it? You even wondered it yourself."

He gripped the steering wheel, and she realized she'd gone too far with that comment. He released a deep breath before he responded. "No, it's not, but now you've dragged me into a lie. I'm not the same person I used to be Kelly. I've changed."

"I heard. You go to church now." She hadn't

missed that piece of information or the way Joanne had seemed to lay claim to him. And why did that bother her so?

"I'm no saint, and I know better than anyone that it's not impossible for him to be mine. But I've been going to church and I've found God. How will I face my church members now with this lie?"

She'd felt something was different about him, and now it all made sense. "I didn't know you'd started going to church."

"Of course, you didn't. You don't know anything about my life anymore."

That stung, but he was right. She hadn't kept up with him. They hadn't even spoken in more than a year before a few days ago. "I don't know what's been happening, but I know you, Zeke. I know your heart, and I'm sure anyone else that knows you knows you would never abandon your responsibilities. You would step up and be a dad to your son."

"But he's not my son, Kelly."

But he could be.

She bit back those words. She was going to have to have a conversation with him about the pregnancy and miscarriage, but not now, not while this was going on.

"I understand if you don't feel comfortable with this. You don't have to do it."

"I want to keep you safe. Truthfully, I'm more concerned with Brady's and your safety than I am with my reputation. I just wanted you to know what was going on with me."

"I'm glad you told me." But she wasn't really. She didn't like hearing that Zeke had become a Christian. It felt like a betrayal somehow. Her family wasn't the only thing she'd run from when she left home.

"Maybe you could come to church with me on Sunday?"

She shook her head. "No, that's not going to happen."

"I don't understand you sometimes, Kellyanne."

"If you've become a Christian, I think that's great for you, Zeke, but it's not for me. I've got enough people trying to run my life as it is. I don't need God telling me what to do, as well."

"That's not really what being a Christian means."

"I'd rather not talk about it," she insisted. She was going to hear enough about God when she saw her family. She didn't need it now too. "Please, just drive me home."

Zeke looked like he wanted to say something else, but she turned her head away and studied the reflection in the window instead of engaging with him. Finally, he started the car and headed for Silver Star.

He accepted her demand for silence for several miles, but once they hit the highway, he spoke again. "I guess I just don't understand why you're so reluctant to return to Silver Star. If I had a family like yours, I'd be happy to see them."

"I'm not unhappy to see my family, Zeke. I love them. But you have no idea what it's like to be the youngest of six kids, and the only girl at that. Growing up like that made me careful about what I do and say. They were always watching me, telling me what to do and lecturing me whenever I made a mistake."

"They love you, Kelly. They were just watching out for you."

"I know, and I appreciate it, but having five older brothers, all of them in some kind of law enforcement, didn't exactly make me the popular girl at school. They were so intimidating to the first boy I ever brought home, he never even spoke to me again."

"Your family is great, Kelly. I'm sure they didn't mean any harm."

"It doesn't matter what they intend. The results are always the same. Every time I come home, I feel like that little girl who has no control over her life. I feel like I'm suffocating. When I'm home, I seem to revert to that role. Everyone has an opinion about my life and how I should live it."

She glanced at Zeke and realized that was why she was drawn to him. He was staunch and protective, but he didn't make demands of her. He allowed her to be a part of the conversation. She knew he'd wanted to insist on her returning to Courtland, but he'd kept it to himself and let her reach that conclusion on her own. It had been the right choice, but it had also been her choice.

"Is that the reason you never brought me home with you?"

"Of course. I couldn't risk letting my brothers run you off, could I?"

His jaw clenched. "I guess I understand that. I just wish you'd told me all this years ago. I thought…" He cleared his throat, and she suddenly had a terrible realization.

"You thought you were the reason I never brought you home to my family."

He tried to shrug it off, but she saw the pain in his expression. "You always wanted to keep our relationship a secret. I thought maybe you were ashamed of me."

"How could you think that?"

"I wanted to be your boyfriend, Kelly, but you kept me at a distance. I would see you and your family around town, and you acted like I didn't exist."

"That had nothing to do with you, Zeke."

"You know I never had much in the way of family. If I had one like yours, I'd consider myself a blessed man. I guess I just can't understand how you can treat what you have—the blessing you have—like something you need to escape from. You may have felt differently if you'd never had one."

The choke in his voice tore at her. He'd had a difficult life being raised as an only child by a grandmother after his parents were killed.

She thought about his words as she watched the landscape open up and the familiar lands appear. She knew them all and most of the names of the families who inhabited them. Zeke looked at what she had and was jealous, but the truth was she was a little jealous of his life. He'd never had anyone watching his every move and critiquing it. He'd had all the freedom to come and go as he pleased and to make his own decisions. He might feel alone in his life, but she couldn't help thinking he took his freedom for granted.

She knew she should be more content with her life. She loved her family. That was never in question. Each of her brothers held a special place in her heart, and she knew they all wanted the best for her. But their methods were sometimes questionable. They didn't always let her make her own decisions. She didn't know if that was just them being big brothers or if it had to do with their law-enforcement brains and training.

Either way, it hurt her to realize how she'd unintentionally hurt Zeke with her behavior.

What a mess you've made, Kelly.

She braced herself as Zeke turned the car into the entrance and under the sign that announced the Silver Star Ranch. Zeke pulled up close to the house and parked. The dogs barked and darted for the car, and, as usual, she felt the pull of familiarity as she glanced at her childhood home. She'd loved growing up here, but each time she returned, she felt like that thirteen-year-old girl under her family's rule.

The front door opened, and her mom and dad exited the house, followed by her brothers Lawson and Paul and their wives, Bree and Shelby.

Her mother spotted her and rushed out to greet her, wiping her hands on her apron. "Kellyanne, we weren't expecting you." Her expression changed the moment she saw the bruises on Kellyanne's face. "What happened?" she asked, pulling Kellyanne into a hug. Kellyanne caught the scent of her mother's face cream. It always reminded her of home.

"I'm fine, but there is a problem, and we felt it would be safer to come here than to stay in Austin."

Her mother frowned and glanced at Zeke, who had removed the car seat and Brady from the back seat of the car. "Is that a baby? Kelly, why is Zeke pulling a baby from your car? For that matter, why is Zeke with you?" Exasperation mingled with the worry on her mom's face, and she saw the rest of her family shared her concerns.

She unlocked the buckles and pulled Brady from the carrier, holding him against her chest. "Everyone, this is Brady." They all stood stunned for a moment, and Kellyanne knew they were thinking Brady was hers and she hadn't told them. They weren't far from the truth, but she quickly filled them in. "Brady is my friend Lisa's son. She died a few days ago. Now he's in danger, and I've promised to keep him safe."

Zeke stepped up beside her. "*We've* promised to keep him safe."

She saw her family's relief, but it gave her an indication of how they might have reacted to her really being pregnant. They would have been shocked, just like they'd been now with Brady, but they would also have been understanding and forgiving, just as they'd all forgiven her brother Miles for his deceptions a few years ago when he'd brought Melissa and her son, Dylan, home and claimed she was his wife. They'd all fallen in love with her and Dylan only to learn that she was his witness and not his wife. Thankfully, things had worked out, and Melissa and Dylan were now truly a part of the family, but the secrets Miles had hidden from them had stunned the family.

Now she was following in his wake. Would they offer her the same forgiveness? Sure they would, but not before they lectured her about her choices.

Her sister-in-law Bree hugged Kellyanne, rubbed Brady's head and looked at him with an awestruck expression. "He's beautiful." Her own belly was round with her and Lawson's first child, Kellyanne's soon-to-be first niece.

"He is, and he's such a good baby. I used to watch him sometimes when Lisa needed to go out, so I've become very attached to him. Now it seems I'm all he's got."

Lawson stepped forward. "Hold on. Something isn't right. Zeke, how did you get involved in all this?"

Zeke's face reddened, but he stepped up. "I went to see Kellyanne when I was in Austin for the law-enforcement conference. I was with her when she found her friend murdered."

Everyone gasped. "Murdered?" her mother cried out and gasped, clutching her chest. "Lisa is the woman who lives next door to you, isn't she?"

Lived. "Yes, she did."

"A murder in your building?"

Zeke interjected. "The detective in charge doesn't believe it was a random killing. They believe she was killed by Brady's father because of something she knew." He looked at Kellyanne, and she understood from his glance that this was the time to tell them everything.

"Lisa left me a voice mail message stating she was going to confront Brady's father. She said she'd hidden evidence of their affair. We believe whoever Brady's father is murdered her to keep her silent."

"What do you know about this man?" Shelby, Paul's wife, asked.

"Almost nothing. She didn't tell me his name. All I know about him is that he's someone of influence, and if anyone finds out about the affair and Brady, it could ruin him. Zeke and I tried to do some investigating, but it hasn't worked out. Once I realized Brady was in danger, I knew I had to get him out of town to keep him safe." She tickled him under his chin, and he giggled, sending darts of love through her. "I can't believe anyone would try to harm him, but I've seen it firsthand."

"What about this evidence Lisa claimed to have?" Lawson asked her.

"She claimed to have a flash drive with evidence, but we haven't found it."

"So maybe the killer took it with him after he killed her?" Bree suggested.

Zeke shook his head. "Maybe, but if he

did, then why would he still want Kelly and Brady? They've both become targets since this started, and we're no closer to discovering why. That's why we thought it would be safer to leave Austin and come here."

"We're glad you did," her mother said, putting her arm around Kelly's shoulders.

Lawson agreed. "You're definitely safer here."

Her father reached out to Zeke and shook his hand. "Thank you for keeping her safe and for bringing her home. I'm glad you were in town when all this happened."

"I'm glad too. I'm sure Josh never expected this when he sent me to that conference. Unfortunately, I missed most of the classes I was there to attend."

"There's something else," Kellyanne told them. "We thought it would be a good idea to keep Brady's identity a secret, so we've decided to tell people that he's my child. Mine and Zeke's."

This time, Zeke's face turned bright red, and he lowered his head and shoved his hands into his pockets, but he didn't refute her. She'd made the decision and dragged him into it, but it was a good decision. She had to do whatever it took to keep Brady safe.

She glanced at her family for their reactions, finally landing on her mother.

After a moment of annoyance, she shrugged and took Brady from Kellyanne. "Why does my family keep bringing me children they pretend are my grandkids?"

Everyone chuckled. This wasn't exactly the same. In that case, Miles had let them all believe Melissa was his wife and Dylan was his stepson. Kellyanne was at least telling them the truth. "It won't be for long," she assured her mother. "Just until this is over."

"I assume this is what Josh wanted to talk to us about," Paul asked.

Zeke nodded. "He should be here soon. He wants to set up a protection detail and then work on discovering who is after Kelly and Brady."

"And Zeke is going to be staying at the house until this is over," Kellyanne added. "We thought it would be best."

"Of course, you're welcome," her dad stated. "We'll fix up a spare room for you."

"Thank you. Once Josh arrives and we have everything settled, I'll head back to my place. I need to check on my animals and pack a few more things."

Brady started fussing, and Kellyanne took

him back. "I really should get him inside and feed him."

"We have a crib set up if you want to use it," Bree said, rubbing her belly. "We won't need it for a while."

"I appreciate that, but I brought his Pack 'n Play. I'll just set that up in my bedroom."

"I'll carry your stuff upstairs," Zeke offered, and Kellyanne thanked him and walked inside with her mother and sisters-in-law while the men unloaded the car.

Zeke was still unloading the trunk when Josh's sheriff truck pulled up. He got out and motioned for his brothers and Zeke to follow him into the barn. Zeke glanced into the house and spotted Kellyanne inside with her parents, Bree and Shelby. She wouldn't like knowing they were discussing her situation without her involvement.

"I'm sorry I wasn't here when Kellyanne and Zeke arrived," he told Lawson and Paul. "I got hung up." He took out his cell phone, pressed a few buttons and two faces popped up—Kellyanne's two remaining brothers, Colby and Miles. "Thanks for joining in," Josh told them.

"No problem," Colby responded. "What's going on with Kelly?"

Josh glanced toward him. "Zeke, why don't you recap what happened back in Austin."

He filled the group in, telling them about finding Kellyanne's neighbor dead, the subsequent attacks on Kellyanne, and Lisa's words that she'd confronted Brady's father.

Paul pulled a hand through his hair. "So we need to figure out who this guy is before he can target Kelly and the baby again."

"Send me the security images of the men from the day care and the stairwell," Colby told them. "I might be able to run them through our FBI facial-recognition system."

Josh nodded. "Cecile and I will follow up with this Detective Shaw to see if he's made any new discoveries and maybe get eyes on his evidence, as well. I especially want to get my hands on Lisa's phone records and examine her social media accounts. We might find a clue there about who she was seeing at the time she became pregnant."

"I think he'd be open to that," Zeke stated. "I'll text you his number." He was glad Josh was bringing Cecile Richardson, his Chief Deputy, in on this. She was always thorough.

"Paul and I have some new cameras we

ordered a while back. We'll get them set up around the ranch just in case there's any trouble," Lawson stated, and Paul nodded his agreement.

"Good. Do that. Zeke is going to be staying at the house, and he'll take point on keeping Kellyanne and the baby safe. We'll all back him up as needed."

Paul shot him a look that said he wanted to know more about why Zeke was hanging around, but Zeke didn't offer up any explanation. Josh hadn't asked for one either, but he was certain he would eventually.

The smart thing to do was to walk away and let her brothers handle this matter now, but he couldn't do it. Just because they weren't together anymore didn't mean he could leave her, not while she was in danger. But the sooner this threat against her was neutralized, the sooner he could untangle himself from this relationship and move on with his life.

After the meeting broke up, everyone left except for Lawson, who locked eyes with Zeke. They had worked together at the sheriff's office before Lawson decided to focus his attention on the ranch, but he still filled in as a deputy as needed for his brother, and

Zeke considered him a friend. The intensity of his stare and the question in his expression made Zeke swallow hard.

He folded his arms and stared at Zeke. "Is there something going on between you and my sister?"

Zeke had been waiting for this question, and he could answer it honestly. "Not anymore."

He probably owed them all more of an explanation, but it wasn't his place to tell them how Kellyanne had hurt him or the weird and complicated aspects of their relationship. That was her secret to tell her family if she chose to.

He headed inside and stowed his bag in the spare room Mrs. Avery had readied for him. He'd always wanted to be welcomed into this house. He'd admired this family for so many years. They'd been good to him, too, and he appreciated that. Kelly had no idea what it was like to grow up alone and poor. Her family always had enough, even with six kids to feed.

His grandmother had worked and scrimped to put food on the table. A bitter taste filled his mouth. His father had ruined them all when he'd killed Zeke's mom and taken his own life. He'd been selfish, only thinking about himself instead of how his mother and child were supposed to survive or what kind of life and scandal he was leaving behind for his only son. Zeke had struggled for so long to shed that stigma, but in a small town like Courtland, memories were long and scandal stuck.

Those resentful feelings flowed through him so easily. It took Zeke several moments and more than one deep, calming breath to push them away. He could wallow in his past or look to his future. That was what faith had given him. A future. He had to choose to cling to it though and not allow his past negativity to rule him. He didn't have to be the poor kid of a killer any longer, not when he was the son of a King.

He cleaned up and walked downstairs to find Kellyanne and her family sitting around the table. Diane Avery was holding Brady, and she seemed to be getting attached to the little guy. He knew from experience it was easy to do. When that kid smiled at him, he tugged at his heartstrings.

"Why is this your responsibility?" her mother asked. "Isn't it your job to place children in a home, not to move them in with you?"

"Brady isn't just some kid, Mama. He's my best friend's child. I used to babysit for him. I feel a greater responsibility toward him."

He noticed John Avery had Lisa's legal papers in his hand and was reading through them. "According to this, she expected you to keep him and raise him."

"I'm not ready for that," Kellyanne protested. "I'll keep him until I can find a good home for him."

"Kellyanne, he's not a puppy," her mother scolded. "He's a child."

"There are a lot of people who can give him a good home." She rubbed his head and a softness overcame her expression. She truly loved Brady. She would be the best mother for him, but she couldn't see it. She didn't see the beautiful, confident woman he saw in her.

She glanced up at him briefly before pain filled her face and she quickly looked away. "I'm not ready to be a mother."

Zeke interrupted them. "I'm heading over to my place. Paul and Lawson are here to keep an eye on you both."

She jumped to her feet and followed him

to the door. Anxiousness was scattered over her face when he turned to her.

"You are coming back, aren't you?" She lowered her head and gave a half-hearted shrug.

He bit back the retort that immediately came to his mind. Leaving and not returning was her thing, not his. "I said I would keep you safe, and I will. I'll be back in a few hours."

"I can come with you."

"That's not necessary."

"I want to go."

"I'll watch the baby for you," Bree offered. "Lawson and I could use the practice."

"Sure, you go," Mrs. Avery suggested. "We'll be fine."

He was conflicted. He wanted to be with her, but he needed to keep his distance. He didn't get a chance to say no. Kellyanne quickly made her way out of the house and hopped into the car. He had to be careful. She'd made it clear she wasn't interested in a relationship with him, and he was already too close for his own good.

He got into the car and headed off. It wasn't until he turned away from town that she commented. "I thought you had a place in town."

"I did, but I moved back to my family's land last year. When my grandma died, she left me the house and the land. I've been working to pay off some of the debt and moved back into the house a few months ago. It still needs a lot of work, but I plan to do it myself."

"I'm sorry about your grandma. I know she loved you."

"Thank you. She loved that ranch. When my dad died, a piece of her died with him. She sold off a lot of the land throughout the years, so there are only a few acres left, but I'm hoping to be able to buy it back and one day reestablish the ranch. It's been in disrepair for years."

"I think she would like that you want to keep the place."

"It's my family home. I want to restore it, turn it back into a working ranch and hopefully raise a family there one day. Maybe even start a legacy like the Silver Star."

"We've sold off our share of land through the years. This place is nothing like the acreage my grandfather used to own."

"Yeah, but it's still yours and your brothers'. It's still family."

"You're wrong about that, Zeke. It's where

I grew up, and it will always be home, but it will never truly belong to me."

"I didn't think you wanted it."

She seemed uncomfortable by the direction of the conversation. "It's my home. How could I not want it?"

He was saved from having to respond by the turnoff onto his property. He drove up to the house and parked. His friend Spencer had agreed to look after his animals—he had two horses in the barn, chickens, and a lazy dog named Howler that he'd found as a stray at the grocery store.

When the car approached the house, Howler leaped from his favorite place on the porch and ran for the car. Zeke parked and got out as the dog danced around his legs until he knelt to pet him. He looked well taken care of it, and he was certain Spencer had tended to the other animals, too, but he would double-check before he left, just in case.

Kellyanne got out of the car and glanced around. "Wow, you've done some work here."

He had. This property had been all but abandoned after his parents died. His grandmother had tried to keep it up, but she'd been grief-stricken and burdened with raising a child all on her own, and Zeke hadn't been old enough to carry the load. After several years, they'd left the ranch and moved to town. It wasn't until after his grandmother had died and he'd inherited this land that he'd turned his attention to reviving it. No matter how hard they'd had it, his grandmother had never been able to bring herself to sell the ranch house and the land around it.

He'd spent a lot of time fixing up the house to make it livable, and he had hopes of expanding it one day to make it large enough to house a family. He'd hoped Kellyanne would want to be a part of that family, but those were the kinds of dreams he'd had to set aside. Kellyanne would never return to Courtland for good. He had to accept that and move on.

She scanned the house, the barn and the shed. His little piece of land was nothing compared to Silver Star, but he had big dreams for it. He expected to see criticism in her face, but instead he saw excitement.

"You should plant some flowers here in front of the house," she told him. "And you could plant a garden toward the back." She walked toward the barn. "How many horses do you have?"

He followed her, happy to see her interest in his property. "I've got two. Right now, that's all I can handle. Once I get this barn rebuilt, I want to add more stalls. I also have plans to get some fences up and raise cattle."

She admired one of the horses, a brown mare he called Sissy. "She reminds me of the horse I had growing up. Her name was Riley. I used to spend hours on her."

He enjoyed hearing her reminisce about a good time she'd had on her family's ranch. It gave him some strange hope that she could possibly be happy in Courtland again.

She stroked the horse's nose and flashed him an endearing smile. "It's a great place, Zeke. It has a lot of potential."

He soaked in her approval. It shouldn't matter so much to him what she thought of his place, but it did. "What other improvements would you make?"

"It's not really my place to say."

But it could be, if only she wanted it. "Tell me. I'd like to know." He touched her hand, still hovering on the horse's nose, and his breath caught as she stared into his eyes. He would make any change she deemed necessary just because she wanted it.

"A big, beautiful back porch would be nice.

You could sit in a rocker and watch the sun set over the pond."

Only if she would sit beside him.

Time seemed to stand still for a moment as he imagined having her with him, rebuilding this ranch and beginning a life together. It was everything he'd ever wanted. He reached to push a strand of her hair from her face, and the gesture sparked something inside of him, something he'd tried his hardest to push away.

He stepped back and broke their connection. Rehashing those dreams wouldn't bring either of them anything but heartache.

"I should head inside and get my things."

He grabbed his bag from the car and headed for the house, and Kellyanne followed him inside. "Make yourself at home," he said as he removed the clothes from the bag he'd taken to Austin with him and tossed them into the washer and then packed fresh, clean clothes. He'd prefer to be here at home, but Kellyanne and Brady were safer with her family surrounding her, protecting her, and he intended to be there too.

"I like what you've done with the place," Kelly said from the kitchen. "You've put some work into it."

He recalled the first time he'd stepped

through the doors as an adult. His friend Spencer had seen a broken-down mess that, in his opinion, needed to be demolished, but Zeke had seen something to be saved and restored. He'd rebuilt where needed, but he wanted to preserve as much as possible. In his mind, that was what God had done for him, taken a broken-down mess and given him new life.

Kelly peeked her head through the doorway as he zipped up his suitcase. "A car is approaching the house."

On an average day, that wouldn't concern him, but ever since he'd met back up with Kelly, nothing had been average, and he wasn't taking any chances.

He removed his gun from the holster, walked to the front door and peered out through the curtain to see a silver sedan he recognized stop. The door opened, and his gut clenched.

Mandy.

The woman who got out had become a good friend to him since he'd joined Courtland City Church and rededicated his life to Christ. She was someone he'd poured his heart out to about Kelly. She would have opinions about finding Kelly here and his involvement in keeping her safe.

His new world and his old world were about to collide right in front of his eyes.

Mandy walked toward the house. He set his gun on an end table. "Wait inside," he told Kelly and then opened the door and met Mandy at the porch step.

"I heard you were back in town. How was the conference?" Her tone was friendly, and she was smiling, but he knew her well enough to see the questions and confusion behind her expression.

He folded his arms and walked down the steps. "You talked to Joanne, didn't you?"

She gave a sigh and nodded. "She called and said she'd seen you. She said you had a woman and a baby with you?" She stared at him and put her hand on her hip. "What's going on with you, Zeke?"

He knew Mandy had a crush on him, and he'd even considered asking her out a few times, but Kellyanne's pull had always kept him from moving on. He had intended to ask her out once he ended things with Kelly and returned to Courtland alone. That hadn't happened.

"I ran into Josh's sister in Austin."

She frowned. "The one you used to date?"

He hated the way her forehead crinkled when he nodded. He didn't want to hurt her.

"Are you back together?"

He didn't know how to answer that, but he obviously hesitated just long enough.

"You know how she treated you, Zeke. Besides, what about your decision to be a better man?"

"I'm trying to be a better man. Her life is in danger, Mandy. Someone is targeting her and her baby."

"Who's the father, Zeke? Joanne said it was you. Is that true?"

He bristled, not caring for her demanding tone. Kelly wanted him to claim Brady was their child, but he couldn't lie…especially not to someone he went to church with. "His mother was Kellyanne's best friend. She was murdered. Josh asked me to convince her to return to Courtland, and she has. Now we have to keep her safe. I'm going to stay at the Silver Star until we figure out who is after her."

Despite his desire not to hurt her, he saw pain flash in her eyes. "I'm worried about you. You have a new life now. Don't let her pull you away from it."

"She won't."

She locked eyes with him. "This is me you're talking to, Zeke. I know how difficult it was getting over her."

He had shared that. He'd been in a dark place over Kellyanne's rejection and determined to make a change in his life. He'd shared that with Mandy and the group of friends he'd made at church. It was no wonder they were questioning how he was helping Kellyanne now.

"This has nothing to do with that, Mandy. She's Josh's sister, and I'm a cop. I have a responsibility to help her."

"You need to be careful. This isn't about jealousy. I'm concerned. We all are after hearing what Joanne had to say. Do you want to go back to how things were before?"

No, he didn't want that. He wanted to move forward, to build a better life. The one he'd been on track to having before he'd gone to see Kelly in Austin.

Mandy's eyes widened as she glanced behind him. He turned and saw Kellyanne standing in the doorway.

She held up her phone. "We need to get back. Mama says the baby is getting fussy."

Irritation burned him, knowing that Kellyanne was showing her jealousy, marking her territory. Well, he wasn't anyone's territory. She was threatened at losing something she didn't even want. Mandy was right. He needed to do a better job of protecting his heart. Just moments earlier, he'd been imagining a future on this ranch with Kelly.

He steeled himself. No more.

"We have to go." He stepped back inside, grabbed his gun and his bag, then locked the door and headed for the car.

Mandy glared at Kellyanne for several moments before walking back to her car, sliding inside and starting the engine.

He didn't want to hurt her feelings. He did care about her and was thankful for her friendship, but he couldn't ignore the threat against Kellyanne. He couldn't believe God would want him too either.

She rolled down her window for one last question. "Will I see you in church on Sunday?"

He sighed, again frustrated. He'd tried to make attending a priority, but lately, things kept getting in the way—his job and the crazy shifts he worked, the conference, now this. "I can't make any promises, but I'll try." That decision was still a few days away. This could all have blown over by then, and he wouldn't have to choose.

Her face was drawn as she put the car into gear and drove away. She would report their conversation to the rest of their group of friends, and he expected to receive several more concerned messages from them. He didn't want to push aside their concerns, but his priority right now was caring for Kelly and Brady. They had to be his number one priority until the threat was taken care of.

He turned to Kelly and sighed, then he motioned for her to get into the car. She did, and he headed back toward Silver Star.

Maybe he could convince her to attend services with him. He shook his head. He had to watch where his mind went. Kellyanne wasn't interested in religion. He was getting ahead of himself, just as Mandy had warned him about.

Being around Kellyanne was dangerous to his heart and to the new life he was trying to lead. They were just headed in different directions.

FIVE

Kellyanne remained silent on the drive back home. She'd been stunned to see another woman show up at Zeke's house. She'd never allowed herself to think that he might be interested in another woman. And she didn't like the green-eyed monster that took root in her.

Zeke was free to date anyone he wanted. She had no ties over him…and never would once he discovered about the pregnancy and how she'd kept it from him.

When they arrived back at Silver Star, she jumped from the car and hurried into the house. Her mother was rocking Brady, and the baby was crying but it wasn't a cry she recognized. Had she traumatized him by leaving him with people he didn't know? He'd already lost his mother. Her heart broke at the thought that he might be afraid she'd left him too.

"He won't settle down," Bree told her. "Your mom and I have tried everything."

"I think he probably just missed you," her mom said, transferring Brady into her arms. "You're the only stable thing he knows since his mom is gone."

Her thoughts again landed on Lisa and finding her the way she had. Brady would never know what a wonderful person she had been and how much she had loved him. Usually, she could get Brady to calm right down, but he continued to fuss and cry.

Her mother put her arm around her shoulder, and Kelly fought to hold back irrational tears as the thought of losing Zeke to someone else pressed against her. "Honey, you have to settle down. He can feel what you feel. If you're upset, he'll be too."

"I'll be fine," she told them both. "I'll take him upstairs and see if I can get him to sleep."

She hurried upstairs and closed herself in her room. She held Brady and tried to comfort him, but it was difficult when she was so upset. It didn't make any sense to her. She didn't want a life here in Courtland with Zeke. She didn't own him, and she'd been away for so long that it didn't make any sense for her to think she had any sway over him.

But it still hurt to think he might have moved on from her.

She did her best to push away all thoughts of Zeke and the incident with that Mandy woman. She had to concentrate on Brady now. He needed her.

She rocked him and sang to him until he finally settled down. She placed him in the portable crib, but he slept fitfully, and she heard him sniffle and cough. When she checked on him later, he was flushed and warm. No wonder he was so fussy. She took his temperature and discovered it was high. Brady was sick and needed to see a doctor.

She hurried downstairs and found Zeke talking with her dad. "The baby's sick. We need to get him to the hospital."

Her mother stepped in from the next room, obviously having overhead Kellyanne. "What's the matter with him?" She hurried upstairs with Kelly to check him out. She felt his forehead and smiled. "Honey, it's just a little sniffle. He'll be fine. Just give him some Tylenol to bring that fever down."

Kellyanne bit her lip, unsure. "I would feel better having him checked out by a doctor."

"I've raised six kids. I know how to treat a baby's fever. All new mothers overreact the first time a baby gets a little temperature. Trust me, I know."

Her mother was probably right, but she didn't want to take any chances with Brady. Maybe if she'd gone to the doctor earlier, her own child would be here now.

She turned to Zeke, who was standing in the doorway to her bedroom, having followed them upstairs. "Please, will you drive us to the ER?"

She hoped he wouldn't dismiss her concerns the way her mother had. She'd acted foolish and jealous earlier, but surely he wouldn't hold that against her, not when Brady needed him.

He didn't hesitate. "I'll meet you downstairs."

Her mother sighed. "All that's going to happen is you're going to waste hours in the emergency room."

"Well, it's my time to waste, Mama. I just want to be sure."

She bundled up Brady and met Zeke outside. He buckled Brady into the car seat, slid into the car and started the engine.

It felt good to have him on her side. It

wasn't a competition, but her mother's comments had made her doubt herself. She should listen to her, but her instincts were telling her to do something else.

Don't listen to your instincts, Kelly. They've led you wrong before.

Remember the baby? You don't know how to care for a child? Listen to those who do.

She pushed those thoughts away. What harm was there in having a doctor examine Brady? Her mother might think she was overreacting, and maybe she was, but she felt better having made the decision to go to the ER.

Zeke reached across the seat and squeezed her hand. "You made the right choice."

She checked on Brady. Zeke was right. His coloring was off and heat radiated from his body. He needed a doctor and maybe an antibiotic.

They raced into the ER, and thankfully, it was a slow night. After only a short wait, the nurse came in and checked him out. "He doesn't seem too bad. Maybe he's a little dehydrated, but that's normal with babies his age. Is he up-to-date on his vaccinations?"

Kellyanne glanced at Zeke, realizing she had no idea how to answer that question. "I—

I'm not sure. I just got him. His mother died a few days ago and I became his guardian."

"Well, he needs to be checked out by a pediatrician." She picked up a chart. "The doctor will be in to see you soon."

She walked out, and Zeke stepped behind her, placing his hands reassuringly on her shoulders. She touched his hands, thankful he was here with her. She glanced at Brady still fussy but trying to sleep. "He's so little, Zeke. How can someone so little have so many problems?"

"He's got you, Kelly. That's one thing in his favor."

She turned and dug her face into his chest. After a brief moment of hesitation, he put his arms around her.

"He has you, too, Zeke. He may not be old enough to know to be thankful for all you've done for us, but I am, and I'm thankful."

She was still in his embrace when the door opened and the doctor stepped into the room. Zeke pulled away from her, and she moved to the bed as the doctor examined Brady and diagnosed a viral upper respiratory infection. He assured her that antibiotics weren't necessary and that Infants' Tylenol should bring his fever down.

"Thank you," Kellyanne told him, grateful for his advice. Her mother would surely notice that it was the same thing she'd told Kellyanne before she left, but she didn't care. She felt better knowing she'd done all she could to make certain he was okay.

The nurse returned and administered the medicine to Brady. "That should make him feel better soon. The doctor says I can go ahead and start on the discharge paperwork. It shouldn't take too long."

"Thank you."

After she left, Zeke pulled two chairs close to the bed, and Kellyanne sat down. She leaned across the bed and covered Brady's hand with hers as he slept. He looked so little and fragile as he struggled to breathe easily, and her heart broke that Lisa wasn't here to comfort him. She'd been such a good mother and had never seemed to doubt herself the way Kellyanne did.

Zeke's hand found hers, and when she looked at him, she saw awe and concern in his expression. "He's so little," he whispered. "So helpless."

"It not fair that he has to grow up without a mother," Kellyanne stated. "It's so unfair."

"Yes, it is." He let out a weary sigh, and

Kellyanne remembered Brady wasn't the only one who had lost his mother.

"You two have that in common," she told him.

"And more."

If they were right that Brady's father had killed Lisa, then he and Zeke definitely had similar origin stories.

His face was grim. "I wish we didn't. At least he has the opportunity to be raised by another mother who loves him."

He was speaking about her. Tears filled her eyes, and she blinked them away. "I—I can't."

He reached for her hand and gripped it. "Kelly, you would be a wonderful mother to Brady. It's obvious how much you care for him."

She did. She'd loved this little boy since the first moment she'd seen him. She'd helped Lisa rock him and care for him since day one, but she could never be a mother to him after how she'd failed her own child.

Zeke didn't know. He couldn't know what a truly terrible mother she actually was.

He pulled his hand away, stood and stretched. "Why don't I go find us some coffee or hit up the vending machine?"

Food sounded good, and she nodded, glad

he was making an excuse to leave the room so she could have a few moments to pull herself together.

"I'll be right back."

She was so thankful he was here with her. She couldn't have endured all this without Zeke by her side, but allowing him to get this close was dangerous to her heart.

The door opened again, and, at first, she thought Zeke must have forgotten something or the nurse had returned with their paperwork. She wiped her face, trying to gather herself together. She didn't look up for several moments, and when she did, she caught only a glimpse of the man standing beside her before he slammed something at her.

She fell off the chair and hit the floor, pain ripping through her head. Her vision blurred, but she fought losing consciousness long enough to see the man scoop up the baby and rush from the hospital room.

Zeke rounded the corner from the vending machine and saw a figure dart out of the exam room where Kellyanne and Brady were. A chill rushed through him as he dropped his newly acquired items and pushed through the door.

The bed was empty, and Kelly was sprawled on the floor. He rushed to her and turned her over. She was breathing, but a gash on her head was bleeding. He pressed the call button and took off after the man who'd grabbed Brady.

She would want him to chase the man even though it meant leaving her. Brady was in danger, snatched by a stranger, and he wasn't going to allow the man to get away with him. He spotted the closing of a side door and rushed through it, close on the kidnapper's heels. Brady was crying as the man ran, and that helped Zeke keep up with his location.

Good job, Brady. Keep it up so I don't lose you.

He ran from the front of the hospital and saw the man. He didn't want to draw his weapon and get into a gunfight with Brady in the mix, so he chased after them on foot. He caught up with the man and grabbed the back of his jacket with one hand and snatched Brady from his arms with the other. The man stumbled but kept going and Zeke didn't pursue him. His first priority was Brady. He glanced down at the baby, who seemed unhurt. He was probably merely frightened by the abduction attempt.

The squeal of tires alerted him to a car screeching to a stop in front of them. The kidnapper jumped into the car, and it took off and disappeared out of the parking lot, taillights shining in the night. Zeke couldn't catch up to the car on foot and by the time he reached his truck, they would be long gone, but he did manage to grab the license plate number.

Zeke tried to soothe Brady as his face scrunched up and he delivered loud, hitching gasps.

"It's okay, little man," Zeke whispered, gently tapping his back to help settle him. Brady was his main concern, and he needed to get him back inside and checked out, and he needed to make certain Kellyanne was okay. Plus, he needed to phone Josh and update him on what had just happened.

This man had brazenly come into the hospital and snatched Brady. How had they known to find Kellyanne and Brady here? How could they have possibly known that Brady would get sick and need to go to the ER? Only one explanation made sense. They had to have been watching them, waiting for an opportunity to strike.

He pulled out his cell phone to call Josh.

He needed to know about this attack, and Zeke would let him attend to the police matters while he went and tended to Kellyanne and Brady. They were targets, and he should have known better than to leave them alone even for a few moments. It was a mistake he wouldn't be making again.

He returned inside. When he walked back into the examination room, Kellyanne was sitting on the bed having the gash on her head tended to by the nurse. They both breathed a sigh of relief when they saw him. Kellyanne jumped up and reached out her arms for Brady.

He gladly handed him over, happy to see them reunited and thankful the men had not gotten away with the child. Brady seemed to calm down once back in her arms, proof of the bond they'd made. Even though she said she intended to find him a good home, he thought Brady had already found one with her. She would be an amazing mother to this little boy if she could only believe in herself the way he believed in her.

"She's going to need stitches on this cut," the nurse stated. "I'll go get the doctor."

An overwhelming sense of gratefulness flooded him that these two were safe, and he struggled to breathe at the idea that someone could snatch them away so easily. He sat beside her and put his arm around her as she held Brady, and she leaned into him as the nurse exited the room. Walking away wasn't an option for him.

He kissed her head and placed his hand over hers and Brady's. He wasn't letting them out of his sight again.

Kellyanne was still in Zeke's embrace when her brother rushed into the room. Josh stopped at the sight of them but seemed to shake off his surprise quickly. "What happened?"

She hated the way it felt when Zeke removed his arms from around her, and it suddenly made her feel very lost and alone with the baby in her arms.

He stood and faced Josh. "I went to the vending machine. When I came back, I spotted a man darting from the room with the baby in his arms. Kelly was unconscious on the floor."

"He hit me with something," she said. She couldn't believe she'd allowed someone to get so close to her. She should have been paying better attention. She'd allowed them to get to Brady. That shouldn't have happened. They were supposed to have been safe here in Courtland, but somehow, whoever was after her had found them.

"I chased him down to the front entrance where I grabbed Brady from his arms. A car approached, and he hopped inside and they took off."

"Did you get a license number?"

"I did." He rattled it off. It amazed Kelly-anne that he could remember that even with all that had happened. "The car was a black four-door Nissan. It had Dallas tags, so I'm guessing it will come back reported stolen."

Josh jotted down all the information and then looked at Kelly. His face held worry, and she felt it pouring off of him. He might act like the tough and capable sheriff, but she knew him to be a worrywart, especially where she was concerned. "Are you okay?"

She wanted to tell him no, she wasn't fine. She'd been clobbered on the head and her child had been snatched from her arms, but that wasn't what he needed to hear. "I will be. He blindsided me, but he didn't do any serious damage." Not like he might have done to Brady. Who knew what nefarious plans they'd had in store for this little guy?

She owed a great debt of thanks to Zeke for getting Brady back. He'd saved Brady. She touched the baby's back. He'd once again fallen asleep in the comfort of her arms. She couldn't lose him. She'd been foolish to let her guard down even for a moment.

This had all been her fault. She'd already lost one child. She couldn't—she wouldn't—lose another. It only reinforced that she needed to start trying to find Brady a permanent home, one with a mother who knew how to care for her child.

"I'll have hospital security pull the surveillance video. Maybe we can identify these men or their car and put some names to these people. Zeke, why don't you come with me?"

She noticed Zeke hesitate and glance her way. Josh must have noticed it, too, because he quickly added, "I've asked security to post someone at the door. They'll be safe until we get back."

Zeke's reluctance was obvious, at least to her, but he agreed. He turned and leaned down to plant a kiss on her forehead. "I'll be back soon," he whispered.

As he walked out with Josh, she cuddled Brady to her and took a deep breath, stunned by how the sight of him walking out the door put a knot in her stomach.

She was growing way too dependent on Zeke, but as she stared down into Brady's face, she knew she wouldn't change anything.

They both needed him.

"What is going on with you and my sister?" Josh asked Zeke as they took the elevator down to the security office.

He wanted to use his go-to answer of nothing, but he couldn't. That wasn't true any longer. Instead, he answered, "I'm not sure."

Josh looked like he wanted to question him further, but they arrived at the basement floor, and the elevator doors opened. Josh stepped out, and Zeke followed him to the security office where they showed their badges and relayed what had just happened to the security officer on duty.

"Yes, the charge nurse called. We've already sent an officer upstairs to stand guard."

"I know. I made sure he was there before we came down here. We need to look at your security feeds. The suspects fled in a black four-door car outside the main doors."

The security guard pulled up the footage and replayed it for them. As Zeke had suspected, the cameras had picked up the man entering the hospital and fleeing it, as well as the car the would-be-kidnappers had sped away in.

"Print that out for me," Josh instructed the security supervisor.

Zeke stared at the image of the man but didn't recognize him. "I'm sure this isn't one of the men who was after Kelly in Austin."

Josh glanced at the images. "Yes, Detective Shaw sent me those photos, and I have to agree. This is a different guy."

Zeke scrubbed a hand over his jaw as he realized this entire situation was worse than he'd expected. "There's only one reason why all these men would be after Kellyanne or Brady."

Josh nodded his agreement, and Zeke knew they were thinking the same thing. "Whoever Brady's father is, he has the money and power to hire multiple people to come after Brady and Kelly."

Lisa had said in her message that Brady's father was powerful and well-connected, and these attacks seemed to confirm that. He had the power to hire men in separate areas of the state to come after them.

"I'm going to send these images to Detective Shaw and see if he recognizes them. I'll also issue a BOLO for the car. If it was stolen, I imagine they'll dump it now that their kidnapping attempt failed. Maybe that will give us some more leads."

Zeke nodded. "That's a good idea. You should also send these to Colby to run through facial recognition."

While Josh was handing out tasks, he gave one to Zeke too. "You stay with Kelly and Brady."

Zeke was glad for the assignment and wondered if Josh realized he would have done so even without the official word from his boss.

They walked back toward the exam room where Kelly had been placed. There was a turnoff before they reached it. Josh stopped there and gave Zeke a nod. "Keep them safe," he told Zeke before he turned and headed out of the hospital.

He needn't have worried. Zeke had no intention of letting anything else happen to Kellyanne or Brady. He was determined to keep them safe.

He heard his phone beep and took it out. It was a text message from Billy Warner, another friend from his group at church asking how things were going. Mandy's and Joanne's concerns were apparently spreading. He was grateful for friends that worried about him, but they wouldn't change his mind about remaining close to Kellyanne and Brady. He was doing the right thing, and he would deal with the fallout later, even if it meant he would nurse another broken heart when Kelly and Brady went back to Austin.

Every time the door to the exam room opened, Kellyanne flinched and tightened her grip on Brady. The baby was sleeping peacefully in her arms, blissfully unaware of the danger he'd been in. But she was aware of it. And aware of how she'd failed him by not being able to fight off the abductor.

That wouldn't happen again.

The memory of waking up on the floor and realizing that Brady was gone still burned inside her. Panic, dread and sorrow had filled her, and it was only when the nurse had told her that Zeke had chased after the man that she'd had some hope.

What would she do without him?

She would be dead, and Brady would be in the hands of a killer.

The door opened, and the nurse entered,

followed by the doctor. "Time to stitch up that head wound."

"I'll hold him for you," the nurse said, reaching out for Brady. Instead of handing him over, Kellyanne tightened her grip on him.

"I'll be right here with him," the nurse assured her, but Kelly was still reluctant. She was grateful when the door swung open again and Zeke entered.

The nurse turned to him. "We need to stitch up her wound but she won't let me hold the baby."

"I'll take him." He took Brady from her arms and planted a kiss on her head.

If she had to let him go, Zeke would keep him safe. "What did you and Josh discover?"

"Not much. He's sending the video feeds to Detective Shaw to examine and putting out an alert for the car. Other than that, we're at a standstill again." He rocked Brady in his arms as the baby fussed and then closed his eyes and fell back asleep, safe in the big man's arms. "We'll be right outside the door while you get fixed up, then I'll take you home."

He looked natural with a baby in his arms. Was there anything cuter than a cowboy with a baby? She longed again to tell him that he'd nearly been a father, that he might have had one of his own, but she couldn't do that. Not when she was relying on him so much.

"He's very good with the baby," the nurse said, giving her some comfort as the doctor stitched up her wound.

Tears pressed her eyes. "Yes, he is." He would have made a wonderful father, but she'd deprived him of that chance.

"I'd like to do a CT scan and have you stay the night for observation," the doctor stated once he'd finished with her stitches. "Since you lost consciousness, I'd like to make certain there's no internal trauma."

"I'm not comfortable doing that," she insisted. "I'd rather go home. My mother was a nurse. She can watch me."

He sighed and then nodded. "Well, I can't force you. Come back if you have any symptoms of nausea, dizziness or confusion. Otherwise, you're both free to go."

Zeke reentered the room, and the doctor repeated his instructions to him before handing her release papers. He transferred Brady to her to carry and kept his hand on her back as they walked to his vehicle. He wouldn't even leave her side long enough to go get the truck. It didn't hurt her to walk, and she preferred having him with her. She didn't want to be left alone again.

They drove home in silence, but Zeke slid his hand across the seat and held hers. She liked it, liked how connected they'd become even if she didn't like the reason for it. Protecting Brady had brought them together. She could already imagine how much it would hurt when he left her once he discovered her secret.

Tears burned her eyes, and she turned to glance out the window. She pulled her hand away to swipe at her wet face. "I can't believe I could be so stupid."

"You didn't do anything wrong, Kelly."

"I shouldn't have taken him to the hospital. My mother was right. He didn't need to go, and I placed us both in danger."

"You trusted your gut," Zeke told her. "There's nothing wrong with that. Besides, if I hadn't agreed with you, I wouldn't have taken you."

She gave him a smile for his attempt at placating her. "Yes, you would have." The truth was she made the decision to go…and it had been the wrong one.

"You and Brady are safe now. That's all

that matters. Plus, we discovered something important."

"What's that?"

His face twisted. "That whoever is after you knows we're in Courtland. They followed us to town and were watching. We have to be even more careful now."

This place had always been safe for her. Not anymore though.

SIX

Zeke parked the car, and Kellyanne picked up Brady and rushed inside. Her mother pulled her and Brady into a hug. "We heard what happened. I knew you shouldn't have gone there."

"You were right," Kellyanne admitted. Of course, she was right. She always was when it came to her kids.

Her mother touched the bandage on Kellyanne's forehead. "Does it hurt?"

"Not much. I was more concerned about Brady than about my head when I regained consciousness."

"Of course, you were. That's a mother's instinct."

She reached to push her mother's hand away. "I'm not his mother." Tears pooled in her eyes because she realized all she wanted was to rescue Brady, to keep him safe, but she kept failing at that.

She hurried upstairs to her bedroom and placed Brady, who was now sleeping soundly, into the portable crib. She heard the front door open and went back downstairs to find Lawson, Paul and Josh entering along with Cecile, Josh's chief deputy. They immediately turned to Zeke, which irritated her. She was here too. Maybe she wasn't a deputy, but it was her life in danger after all.

"What did you find?" Zeke asked.

Josh shook his head. "Not much. We haven't been able to identify the man who tried to abduct Brady based on the image from the security video. I sent it to Colby to see if the FBI might be able to do better. He'll get back to us if it does."

"What about the car they got away in?" Zeke asked.

"Stolen," Cecile confirmed. "From Dallas two days ago. We do have reports of seeing it in town yesterday."

Kellyanne felt all the blood drain from her face at Cecile's words. "They've been watching us for a while."

Josh folded his arms and looked at her. "That's what we believe."

"We were supposed to be safe here, but we're still in danger."

Zeke took her hand and held it. "I know it's not ideal, Kelly, but we are safer here. They won't try anything with all your family here."

Paul spoke up. "Lawson and I will start patrolling the perimeter. No one will get close to the house. We'll make sure of it."

Bree came and wrapped her arms around Kellyanne. "Don't you worry. We'll all make sure nothing happens to Brady. This is what family is for, right?"

Kellyanne was grateful for their encouragement and security, but she was scared. Cecile was the only one who didn't seem sure of the plan. Kellyanne knew her well enough to see the doubt in her face. "What are you thinking, Cecile?"

"It's obvious they know you're here, and there have been attacks here before. The guys can guard the house, but I still think it would be better if they didn't know where you were."

"My grandfather had a fishing cabin out by the river," Zeke offered. "It's been abandoned for a while, but I went out there a few months ago to clean it up. It's isolated. No one would find us unless they knew where to look."

Kellyanne glanced at him, tears pressing against her eyes. "Would you go with us?"

"Absolutely. I can't let you and Brady out there alone, Kelly."

She instantly felt better knowing that Zeke was on her side. She hadn't managed to completely push him away. At least, not yet.

He nodded and squeezed her hand before turning back to the others. "The road washed out years ago, but I was able to access it on horseback."

Josh rubbed his chin. "I don't like the idea of not being able to get away in a vehicle if needed. Plus, I'd still like Kellyanne around here. If we're going to figure out who Brady's father is, we might need her knowledge about Lisa's life."

Cecile agreed. "Let's call that plan B. For now, I say we just sit tight and make sure they're both protected here at Silver Star."

Kellyanne gritted her teeth in irritation that they were all making plans without even consulting her.

"Don't I get a say in what happens to me?"

Zeke rubbed a hand through his hair. "Kelly, we're not making plans without you. We're just brainstorming ideas."

"I'm the one in danger."

Lawson gave a loud frustrated sigh. "Then tell us what you want to do."

"I don't know," she admitted. They were looking at her as if she were being unreasonable, but she didn't think it was too much to ask to be consulted about her own life. "But that doesn't mean I don't want to be a part of the conversation."

Josh shot her a look she recognized as his let-me-take-care-of-it face. "We'll head back to the sheriff's office and go over the files Detective Shaw sent. Maybe we can locate something he missed." He slipped his hat onto his head. "I'll call if we find anything."

Her brothers left, and Kellyanne fell onto the sofa and covered her face with her hands. "I don't understand how this is happening. How did I let this happen?"

"You didn't let anything happen," Zeke insisted. He walked over and sat beside her, his arm on her shoulder. "You were looking out for your friend and her child. No one can fault you for that."

"I just want to keep him safe. What can I do to keep him safe?"

"Trust me. Trust your family. We're all on your side, Kellyanne. Don't push us away when all we want to do is help you."

"He's right." Her mother appeared in the doorway, obviously having heard Zeke's statement. "Let your brothers do what they know how to do. We all only want what's best for you." She shook her head. "I wish we'd never allowed you to go off to Austin alone, then maybe this wouldn't have happened."

"I'm an adult, Mother. I make my own decisions. Besides, if I hadn't, I wouldn't have Brady. I'm grateful to have known Lisa, and I'm thankful to have him. Who would have watched out for him if I hadn't been around?"

Her mother shook her head. "I suppose you're right, but it doesn't make me feel any better to know my own baby is in trouble."

Kellyanne's cheeks burned. "I am not a baby."

"Kelly, I didn't mean—"

She'd had enough of people planning out her life. "You always do that. I'm not a little girl, Mom. I'm a grown woman now. I won't have anyone making decisions for me or for Brady." She turned and fled up the stairs, leaning against the wall at the top as tears slid down her face.

Below, her mother's words filtered up the stairs. "She's so stubborn. She always has been. I raised five boys, and not one of them gave me the trouble she did." Her mother's words stung, but she couldn't deny the truth in them. She had always been one to defy the rules.

"She is stubborn," Zeke agreed, and those words hurt worse than her mother's. But his next words soothed her. "But she's strong, too, and that's important."

"Take care of her, Zeke. You're the only one who can seem to talk any sense into her. Please keep my daughter safe."

"I will. I promise I'll keep her safe."

Kelly couldn't listen any longer. She hurried to her room and shut herself inside. She couldn't allow her brothers and Zeke to put their lives at risk for her forever. Josh had been right when he'd stated that she was the one who knew Lisa the best. She should be the one to figure out who Brady's father is.

She hurried to her computer and pulled up the social-media site that had images of the fundraiser she and Lisa had attended the night before she'd died. If only she could identify the man who'd threatened her friend. Then they could find their answers.

Zeke slipped on his cowboy hat and walked outside on the pretense of needing to get something from his truck. But what he really needed was a moment to compose himself. Having Kellyanne's mother ask him to watch out for her meant something. This family was accepting him as a part of Kellyanne's life. They weren't judging him for his upbringing or for being the son of a killer. They accepted him and that made him feel worthy.

He walked out and met up with Paul and Lawson, who were getting ready to patrol the area. With Kelly and Brady safely locked inside the house, he offered to help.

"I think it's a better idea if you remain close to the house," Lawson told him. "Just in case."

He agreed and watched them ride off. He would much rather be out there doing something instead of sitting here alone.

He walked back to the front porch and slid into a rocker. He loved the quiet nights here. It was nothing like the big city where he'd lived for six months before returning to Courtland. Country life was for him, not the hustle and bustle of the city. And he loved the night sky. He felt close to God at times like these.

Lord, please help me keep them safe.

He sat for hours soaking up the night before he heard a rustling and got up and walked to the end of the porch. Something wasn't right. He felt it in his bones. He walked off the porch and rounded the barn, stopped by the stunning sight before him.

The pasture was on fire.

Shouting pulled Kellyanne from a deep sleep. At first, she couldn't even remember where she was, but when the shout repeated, her fuzziness cleared.

She jumped from the bed, ran to the window and peeked out. Smoke filtered into the sky above the barn. Her brothers were pulling on their boots and coats, preparing to hurry out.

A fire meant one thing—all hands were needed to battle it before it spread. She dressed quickly, pulled on her boots and went to grab Brady from the portable crib.

She rushed downstairs and saw Lawson and her father pulling on their boots and coats. She grabbed hers, too, and then grabbed Brady's jacket.

"You can't take him out in that, Kellyanne. I'll stay here with him," her mother said from where she stood in the kitchen doorway.

She didn't like being separated from him.

"He can stay in the truck. He won't be near the fire."

"Sweetie, it's so late, and he needs his rest. You go help your brothers. He'll be fine."

Kellyanne battled with herself. She didn't want Brady out of her sight, but her mother was right. It was late, and he needed sleep, especially after all he'd been through. Why wake him when she didn't need to? She was being silly. She trusted her mother to watch after Brady.

She nodded, slipped on her coat and boots, and ran outside to the truck. She slid in beside Zeke as he started off toward the pasture. They were following behind her brothers when Kellyanne heard the dogs barking. She glanced behind them and realized the dogs hadn't followed them. That, in itself, was odd.

She turned around in the seat and saw them rushing back toward the house. A feeling of dread she couldn't explain filled her. "Stop the truck," she told Zeke.

He looked at her. "Why?"

"I have to go back. I can't explain it. I just need to go back to the house to make sure Brady is okay."

His jaw clenched, but he turned the steering wheel. "We'll both go."

She liked that he trusted her without argument. She couldn't give a reason for this feeling. If Brady were hers, she might call it motherly instinct.

The dogs were barking and scratching at the house when Zeke parked. He reached for the rifle at his feet, and she sensed he was now on edge too. They got out of the truck, and she headed for the house, but Zeke grabbed her elbow and pulled her back.

"Wait here." He pushed his phone into her hands. "Call your brother. Something isn't right."

She dialed Josh's number, and he answered on the first ring. "I'm on my way. Paul called me about the fire."

"Josh, come to the house first. Something is wrong."

"What is it?"

"I'm not sure yet. Just come."

The dogs were howling, and he must have heard them, because his response was rapid. "I'll be there in less than five minutes."

She ended the call and hurried to follow Zeke as he approached the house. As they neared it, she heard screaming, and the front door burst open. A man plowed down the steps, Brady crying in his arms. Suddenly, a rifle fired, and Kellyanne screamed. Her mother appeared at the door, rifle in hand, firing high at the intruder, but he didn't stop running. He ducked into the brush and vanished.

"Check on your mother," Zeke ordered as he took off after the intruder.

She ran to her mother, realizing that her lip was bleeding, and she was limping. "What happened?"

"He broke into the house and grabbed the baby. When I tried to fight him off, he shoved me down the stairs and ran out. That's when I went after the rifle. I fired high so I wouldn't hit Brady. I was hoping to scare him, but he didn't stop."

"Zeke has gone after him."

She helped her mother to the rocking chair before rushing inside to get a rag for her. Her thoughts were of Zeke and wondering if he would find Brady. *God, please let him be okay. Don't let that strange man hurt him.* He must be so scared. The sound of his cries as the man ran off with him echoed through her mind.

She returned to her mother, who accepted the cold rag. "Kellyanne, go after Zeke. You have to find him and Brady."

Glad for the reprieve, she reached for the rifle her mother had dropped and hurried off down the lane in the direction Zeke had taken.

She spotted a car coming up the drive and stopped when Josh slammed on the brakes and leaped out. "What happened?"

"A man broke into the house. Mama tried to fight him off, but he shoved her and took off with Brady. Zeke chased him into the brush." She pointed in the direction the men had gone.

Several shots fired from the direction she'd just pointed, and she jumped, startled. Her heart dropped into her stomach. If something had happened to Zeke or Brady... She couldn't go there. She couldn't think that way.

Josh didn't hesitate. He took the rifle from her hand. "Stay here," he told her as he rushed into the brush toward the gunshots.

Kellyanne bit her lip. She didn't like being relegated to waiting to see what happened, especially when it concerned Brady. It was her responsibility to care for him, her job to make certain he was safe.

Unable to wait a moment longer, she darted into the tree line and followed the sound of voices to a clearing. She crouched down when she heard shouting and crying. The man held Brady with one arm and held a gun with the other. If he fired the gun that close to Brady, it would hurt his little ears for sure. She had to do something.

Zeke and Josh stood on the other side of the clearing. Both had their weapons raised at the ready and had cornered this man. They hadn't seen her yet, and neither had the assailant. She was so close. If only she could grab Brady and run. She could do it before he even realized she was there. The man was screaming at Zeke and Josh to put down their guns or else he would hurt Brady. Between his hollering and Brady's wails of terror, her movements would be difficult to hear.

She inched toward him. She dared a glance at Zeke and realized he'd spotted her. He gave her an ever-so-slight shake of his head, trying to warn her off, but she couldn't stand Brady's crying any longer. She had to act now.

She reached out for him and pulled him from the man's arms, hugged him to her, then turned and took off running all in one swoop. The man swore and spun to grab her. Shots fired a moment later, and then she heard Zeke and Josh yelling. She didn't stop. She kept running until she realized no one was chasing after her.

She took a moment to soothe Brady, who was already starting to settle down as she cradled him and pressed him against her. When his wails turned to whimpers, she took a chance and walked back toward the clearing, anxious to learn what had happened.

The man was on the ground, his hands in cuffs, and a jacket pressed against a bleeding wound on his shoulder.

"Let's get him to the car," Josh said as he and Zeke helped the man to his feet.

Zeke spotted her and left Josh with the assailant. He ran toward Kellyanne and his strong arms went around her and Brady. She soaked up his embrace.

"I wish you hadn't done that," he groaned. "I nearly died when I saw you."

She felt the tension and fear in him and looked up into his face. "I had to do something. I had to get Brady away from him. And it worked."

"Yes, it worked." He turned back to the man Josh was leading past them. "Maybe now we'll get some answers."

He put his arm around her as they walked

back to the house and Josh loaded the kidnapper into the back of his car.

"He probably started the fire as a distraction," Josh stated. "He reeks of gasoline."

She remembered the fire. "Has anyone heard any news?"

Josh pulled out his phone. "I'll call and find out. For now, let's head back to the house and check on Ma."

Josh drove to the house while she and Brady walked with Zeke.

"Thank you," she whispered as they walked.

"For what?"

"For believing me when I thought something was wrong. I don't know what I would have done if he'd managed to get away with Brady."

"Well, he didn't. Besides, you were right. Something was wrong." He stopped and stroked Brady's cheek. "His mother was right to have you watching out for him."

Her heart swelled with affection at him saying that, but she wasn't alone. "He has us both, Zeke. Without you, we wouldn't be safe." She hoped, she prayed, that wouldn't change.

He must have noticed the question in her eyes, because he was quick to reassure her.

"I'm not going anywhere, Kelly. I'm here for you and Brady for as long as you need me."

She leaned into him, grateful for his declaration. She'd been worried when they'd arrived at the ranch that he might keep his distance because she had her brothers around. She felt better with him here. Plus, he knew what they'd been through in Austin, and he didn't try to make decisions for her the way her brothers did.

Sirens wailed, and she turned and spotted two police cruisers and an ambulance zoom down the lane toward the house. It sent her mind back to her mom, who had been shoved down and hurt. She handed the baby over to Zeke, who took him willingly, and then she rushed to the house after the vehicles.

Although she arrived moments after the ambulance, the paramedics were already examining her mother and recommending she go to the hospital.

"I'm fine," she insisted. "It was just a bump, that's all."

Josh paced around her. "I think you should go have it looked at."

Kellyanne sat on the step beside her mother. "I think that's a good idea, Mom. He hit you pretty hard."

"I won't leave while the pasture is on fire and someone is after this child. I promised to protect him, and I let you down, Kelly."

"You didn't let me down. Brady is safe. See for yourself." She motioned to Zeke approaching the house with Brady in his arms. "You did everything you could to protect him."

"It wasn't enough." She reached out to Kellyanne's face and tucked a strand of hair behind her ear with a shaking hand. This incident had frightened her. "If you hadn't come back, I don't know what would have happened to him. Why did you come back?"

"It was all Kellyanne," Zeke replied. "She felt like something was wrong and made me turn around."

"Not really," she insisted. "I was prepared to walk back."

Her mother stared at her and smiled. "I'm glad you trusted your instincts."

She was too. The thought of what might have happened to Brady shook her. She couldn't explain the need to turn around to check on him, but she was happy she'd trusted that gut feeling. For once, her instincts had been right. And to have her mother realize it as well was just the topping on the cake. "Me too."

Josh handed off the intruder to Cecile. "Get his shoulder checked out then book him. I need to get to the field to see about the fire."

"I'll go with you," Zeke stated, transferring Brady to Kellyanne's arms.

"I'll leave Martin here until we return," Josh stated, motioning toward one of the deputies who'd arrived with Cecile. "We won't be long."

Kellyanne hugged Brady to her and sat in the rocker. He was settling down, but he'd had quite a fright. She rocked him until he nodded off. She glanced at her mother, who smiled at her.

"You're good with him."

"I don't feel like it. I feel like I don't know what I'm doing most of the time."

"That's how all mothers feel."

She stared, stunned by her mother's words. "Mom, he's not my child. I'm not a mother. Even if I were, I don't think I would be that good at it."

"Kelly, being a mother isn't something that comes naturally. It's something you learn. Brady may not be your child, but you've given him the gift of love and care, and that's the first gift of motherhood. When it happens for you, and I know it will one day, you'll be a wonderful mother."

Tears sprang to her eyes. They were the words she'd longed for so long to hear from her mother, that her decisions were right and good, but Kellyanne was reminded that even though Brady was safe, she'd already had her chance at motherhood and ruined it.

"Kellyanne, what's the matter? You're in tears. Why? What's happened?"

She quickly tried to brush them away and hide her face, but her mother's perception was eagle-eyed. "Nothing. It's nothing."

"It's something." She stared off into the distance. "Is it Zeke? Did something happen between you two?"

Her mother liked Zeke. The whole family did, and she was certain her mom would be glad to learn that something was happening between them. Kellyanne had considered that, even wanted it, but she knew it would never happen, not once he learned about the miscarriage.

"No, nothing has happened with Zeke. And nothing ever will."

"I'm no fool, Kelly. You came here with him and wanted everyone in town to believe this was his baby. Something must have happened between you."

"Maybe once there was, but not now."

"He's a good man, Kellyanne, and it's clear he's in love with you. And I can tell you have strong feelings for him. What's holding you back?"

She wanted so much to confide in her mom about getting pregnant and losing the baby, but she couldn't bring herself to tell her. She couldn't bring herself to tell anyone how much of a failure she was at motherhood. Why would anyone want her to take care of their child?

"I need to put Brady down," she said, standing and walking into the house before her mother could ask any further questions.

No, a future with Zeke was out of the question. She felt a real connection forming between them. He might want her now, but he would never want her when he learned she'd miscarried their baby and hadn't told him she was pregnant to begin with. Plus, she wasn't certain she could care for one child and she was certain Zeke would want a large family. She'd lost her chance with him for good. No point in pining over something she could never have.

She placed Brady into the crib and covered him. He fell back asleep after fussing for several minutes of not being in her arms. She sat on the bed and stared at him sleeping so peacefully. He had gunmen after him and had been nearly been kidnapped, but now he was sleeping without a care in the world because he assumed he was safe with the people who loved him.

She longed to claim him, but she could never give him a good life. Motherhood was not for her, and he would never have a family of brothers and sisters with her.

She sighed and whispered a prayer of thanks for his safe return and that Zeke and Josh had captured the man responsible. Hopefully, now they could get some answers about who was after her and how they had tracked them to Courtland.

Zeke helped the family extinguish the fire, which had turned out to be nothing but a distraction to get them all away from the house so the assailant could abduct Brady. He returned to the house with the brothers, showered, and then checked on Kellyanne and Brady, who were sleeping soundly.

Josh had left two of his deputies on guard

duty at the house, so Zeke felt comfortable enough returning to the sheriff's office while everyone else was asleep. He was anxious for more information on the man he and Josh had captured.

Cecile was interrogating the guy in the interview room, but from what he saw, the man was tight-lipped and offered up nothing. Frustration flowed off her as she exited the room and ordered the man returned to his cell.

"Did he give you anything?" Zeke asked her.

"Not much. He won't say who hired him to kidnap the child."

"You think someone hired him?"

"From what I can tell, he has no reason to target Brady. Child abduction hasn't been his thing. He has no priors for sexual deviance or violence against children. His name is Thomas Stanford. He's a petty criminal from Fort Worth. According to his prints, he's been in and out of jail since he was a teenager. He's a thief and a small-time gambler. Everything he does is for a payout. No doubt someone put him up to this."

Zeke folded his arms and sighed, his brain trying to wrap itself around this. "Lisa's message said that Brady's father is a powerful and influential man. So what's that? A CEO? Oil tycoon? Politician? Thomas Stanford doesn't look like he would associate with anyone like that."

Cecile nodded. "Men with that kind of money and power don't do their own dirty work, Zeke. They have it done for them. And Stanford is just the type of man they might hire." She gave his arm a reassuring nudge. "Don't worry. I'll keep after him. He'll eventually tell me everything he knows."

He trusted Cecile. She was one of the best in the department at interviewing suspects and getting answers, but he couldn't just sit by and let things happen around him. He needed to feel useful. He pulled up the recording of Cecile's interview with Stanford and watched it, looking for anything they might have missed. After viewing it several times, he conceded she'd dug into every possible trail, but Stanford hadn't given up any information.

When morning broke, he called Kellyanne's phone, but she didn't answer, so he phoned the house and discovered she was still sleeping. Good. She needed her rest. She was so worried about Brady, and now her mother had been injured too. It was too much to shoulder, and he wished he could take some of it from her. If only she would let him.

He was deep into looking back through Lisa's telephone records hours later when Cecile rapped on the door to the conference room where he was working. "You need to come now."

Her tone told him something was happening. He jumped to his feet and hurried to the front of the office to find Josh standing at the front desk, a hard expression on his face. A man wearing a suit and carrying a briefcase stood opposite him.

"What's going on?" Zeke asked.

"This is Mr. Stanford's lawyer," Josh told him. "He's refusing to allow us to question his client any further, and he's paying his bail. The judge set the amount twenty minutes ago. Mr. Emmerson didn't blink." He handed Zeke the man's business card, which identified him as Michael Emmerson, an attorney at a big law firm out of Dallas.

The idea that a petty criminal like Stanford could afford a lawyer like this was ludicrous. Someone else had to be paying his bills…someone like the man after Kellyanne and Brady.

"You can't let him go," Zeke demanded.

"You know we'll never see him again, never get the opportunity to question him further."

Josh turned to look at him, his expression tight and his jaw clenched. "We don't have a choice. We have to let him go."

He walked back to his office as a deputy brought Stanford into the room and removed the handcuffs. Stanford gathered his belongings and headed for the door with his attorney, turning to give Zeke a final nod as he walked to his freedom.

It seemed like Kellyanne had only laid her head on her pillow for a few minutes when Brady's whimpers woke her. When she glanced at the time, she realized she'd slept for hours. The sun streamed in from the window, and she heard movement from downstairs.

She got up and glanced into the playpen and saw Brady playing with his teddy bear, giggling and smiling. His grin widened when he spotted her, and he reached for her.

Her heart swelled at the simple gesture, and she picked him up and cradled him. "Hi there, sweetheart. How are you feeling today? Better?"

His sniffles seemed better, and he wasn't

running any fever. The multiple attempts to snatch him hadn't affected him health-wise, and she couldn't help hoping he'd transferred his cold to the men who'd grabbed him.

She carried him downstairs and was glad to see her mother up and about too, but she was sporting a busted lip and a bruise on her cheek. She wasn't moving as quickly as she usually did, but she smiled when she spotted them and reached for Brady. Kellyanne couldn't help but notice how attached her mother had gotten to him in such a short time. They all had.

Bree walked out of the kitchen and stood beside Kelly, watching her. "She's been so worried about that little boy. Lawson and I both told her she needs to take it easy today, but you know how stubborn she can be. I'll make sure she doesn't do anything too strenuous."

Kellyanne hugged her sister-in-law. "I love how much you care about my mother. I'm so happy you're here with her."

"I'm the thankful one. She took me in and treated me like one of her own children. I'm blessed to be a part of this family. I know she feels better having you home, even under these circumstances." She heard cars pull up in front of the house and looked out and gasped. "I'd better finish getting breakfast ready. Everyone is already here."

"What's going on?" Kellyanne asked.

"That's right, you don't know. That man they arrested last night, some high-priced lawyer arrived this morning and bailed him out."

"They let him go?"

"Not by choice. According to what Lawson told me when he got off the phone with Josh, no one was pleased. So Josh called a family meeting here to try to figure out what to do."

The door opened, and Josh, Lawson, Paul and Zeke filtered inside. They removed their coats, boots and hats. Zeke smiled when he spotted her mother with Brady, then walked over to Kellyanne. "How are you this morning?"

"Better. What about you? Did you get any sleep?" She knew he'd been out fighting the fire and then at the sheriff's office seeing about the assailant. He couldn't have slept much, if at all.

"I'll grab a couple of hours once we're done here."

Everyone gathered around the table and helped themselves to the meal Bree had prepared. They'd shared many meals around this table and had held many important conversations.

Kellyanne glanced at Josh. "I heard you had to let him go."

He stared at her, nodded and looked away. "We didn't have a choice. Unfortunately, we weren't able to get any information about who he's working for before he got into his attorney's car. He's probably skipped town."

She glanced at Brady and realized he was still in danger. "What do we do now?"

Josh heaved a sigh and pushed his plate away. "Plan B. We transport you, Brady and Zeke to Zeke's grandfather's fishing cabin."

"Is that necessary?" her father asked Josh. "That seems extreme."

"The people who are after Kelly and Brady know where they are. The only way we have to keep them safe is if they don't."

Paul nodded. "I'll work on some diversions to cover their getaway. We don't want to lead whoever might be watching to where they're going."

Zeke turned to Kellyanne. "How do you feel about going to the cabin?"

It meant so much to her that he'd asked, especially since no one else had even thought to. "I don't like it, but I'll do whatever I need to do to keep Brady safe."

He accepted her answer and turned back to Josh. "We'll uses horses to get there since it's inaccessible by road."

"That'll mean no one can sneak up on you in a vehicle and make a fast getaway," Lawson stated. "That could work in our favor."

Paul grabbed a piece of bacon and bit into it. "I'll start gathering supplies and get the horses ready. We'll drive them over to Zeke's farm, and you can leave from there."

"That's a good idea," Josh stated. "Let's meet back here later this afternoon. I want to make certain everything is ready to go. We'll head out at first light tomorrow morning."

Kellyanne didn't relish the thought of running and hiding, but she trusted Zeke and her brothers, and she was willing to do whatever it took to keep Brady out of harm's way.

She helped Bree clean up the breakfast dishes while the others went to start gathering supplies. She could have left Brady with Bree and gone to help, but she didn't want to leave his side again.

Zeke disappeared into the spare bedroom and got some sleep, but Lawson stuck around to make certain they were safe. She was thankful to have some time to spend alone with Lawson and Bree. She and Lawson had always been close, being the two youngest children of the family. And she'd grown to love Bree after seeing the love and affection she held for her brother and her family. She glanced at Bree's burgeoning belly and knew her brother and sister-in-law were going to make wonderful parents.

Paul and Shelby were expecting, too, although Shelby was not as far along as Bree. Several of her brothers had settled down and were starting families. She envied them. Was she ready for that step in her life?

She hadn't felt ready, not until she'd felt life growing inside of her. But she'd blown her chance for happiness and a family when she'd lost her baby. Having Brady felt like a second chance to her. Could she take it? She'd already fallen in love with this little guy. And he wasn't the only one she'd fallen for.

The moment he entered her thoughts, Zeke seemed to appear. He'd only slept a few hours, but he looked refreshed. He kissed her and then knelt down to play with Brady, who was on a blanket on the floor.

She watched him and couldn't help smiling.

Her mother put her hands on Kellyanne's shoulders. "He's really good with Brady."

"Yes, he is. He cares about him."

"He cares about you too."

She wanted to believe that. She wanted to believe they could have a future together, but everything seemed so messed up. Did she even dare to hope it could happen for them, that she wouldn't mess it up again?

The front door opened, and Paul stepped inside, followed by two of the family's dogs. Kellyanne spotted both dogs hightailing it toward the blanket where Brady lay. "The baby's on the floor," she cried out to Paul.

Zeke swooped up Brady just as the dogs reached them, but one of them grabbed the teddy bear from the floor and darted back out through the door. Brady's face scrunched up, and he cried at having his favorite toy stolen from him, or possibly from the sound of her yelling.

"Grab him," Kellyanne hollered, but he slipped through Paul's arms and fled back through the door.

She hurried after him, calling his name and trying to coax him back. Brady loved that teddy bear, and if the dog ruined it, he would be devastated.

She hurried down the steps and toward the barn where the dog had taken the toy. "Where are you, Radar?" She found him in a corner, pulling and tearing at the stuffing. "Get away from that," she shouted, and the dog dropped the toy and bolted.

Kellyanne walked over and picked up the toy. She fingered it in her hand. The stitching was ripped and needed to be sewed. It was nothing she couldn't handle. As she pushed some stuffing back into the hole, she felt something hard inside. *What is that?*

She dug into it and pulled out a cylindrical object. A flash drive was tucked inside Brady's stuffed bear.

Her heart hammered against her chest, and Lisa's words flooded back to her about the evidence she'd collected. She'd obviously placed it inside Brady's stuffed bear.

They'd had the evidence they needed to discover who was after them all along.

Footsteps behind her caused her to spin around. Zeke was hurrying toward her. "I thought you might need some help." He eyed the toy in her hand. "You found it."

"I found more than this toy." She held up the flash drive and suppressed a squeal of exhilaration. "It was inside the bear. Lisa must have sewn it into the toy and left it in his bag. She knew we wouldn't go anywhere without it."

His face lit up. "We need to find out what's on this. This could be the key to discovering who is after you and Brady."

"My computer is upstairs."

He grabbed her hand, and they ran back to the house and shared the news of what they'd discovered with her parents and Bree. Kellyanne then hurried upstairs, retrieved her computer and set it up at the kitchen table.

Her heart raced with excitement as she pushed the flash drive into the port. This was it. They were about to discover the answer to the biggest question they'd had throughout all of this. Who was Brady's father?

The computer loaded and opened up images of Lisa and a man she recognized.

Kellyanne gasped.

Her friend hadn't been joking when she'd said Brady's father was a powerful figure.

SEVEN

Zeke could hardly believe what his eyes were seeing. He recognized the man in the photo. How could they not?

"Is that—?"

"I think it is," Kellyanne stated. "Senator Walter Davenport."

The intimate photos left little doubt that there was more between Lisa and this man than simple friendship. They weren't racy, but they were intimate and candid shots of the two of them smiling, kissing and laughing together.

He was a family-values senator currently gearing up to run for governor of Texas. You couldn't get much more powerful and influential around here than that. And now he was embroiled in a scandal involving an extramarital affair and an illegitimate child.

Zeke sighed and scrolled through the other

information on the flash drive. Emails with intimate conversations between Lisa and this mystery man as well as dates, times and meetup locations. Lisa had provided them with everything they needed to identify this man as Brady's father except for his name on a birth certificate.

Zeke phoned Josh to update him about what they'd found, and it wasn't long before he joined them at the house. He, along with Paul, Lawson, Bree, and Mr. and Mrs. Avery, scanned the information they'd found.

John Avery whistled in disbelief. "Isn't his campaign all about family values?"

Josh nodded. "The discovery of an illegitimate child would devastate his campaign and probably derail his plans to become president one day. It's no wonder he wanted Lisa and Brady to disappear."

"And now Kellyanne, because she knows the truth too," Bree stated.

Josh shook his head. "Kellyanne was probably only in danger because they suspected she had it. Without this documentation, she couldn't prove anything. No judge would compel a paternity order without proof of the affair."

Paul stood back and rubbed the back of his

neck. "Are we really saying Senator Davenport fathered a child with your friend, then killed her, and now is trying to kill a child?"

Zeke could see Paul was having a difficult time comprehending this. So was he. He'd never expected someone as powerful as Davenport was Brady's father. He'd figured the guy was married, but not a powerful politician. Someone like that knew how to get things done, and he wouldn't stop until he got what he wanted. He wouldn't stop until this threat of exposure was ended.

What had Lisa gotten Kellyanne involved in?

"I think it's safe to say he's involved in all this based on the information on the flash drive," Zeke commented. "Whether or not he's Brady's father or was involved in her death, he certainly had an affair with her. That in itself might be enough to end his career."

Paul shook his head. "A sex scandal with a woman who was murdered would surely do it. No wonder he's trying to cover his tracks."

Kellyanne looked at her brothers and then at Zeke. "So what do we do with this information? Take it to the police? The news?"

"We should at least call Detective Shaw and update him," Zeke said.

Josh agreed. "I'll take care of letting him know, but I want to make sure Kelly and Brady are safe before I do. I appreciate he has a job to do, but our first priority is keeping them safe. Once they're away, I'll call him."

"We have to be very careful," John stated. "This information is monumental, and it could have grave consequences for us all. If this man is involved, he's got powerful friends. They might cover for him or even get him acquitted. We need to have more than proof of an affair before we go public with this information. We need to know if he's involved in your friend's death."

"I'm leaning toward Davenport having all the answers we need," Zeke insisted. "I say we confront him." He was tired of all the running and hiding. Now that they finally had someone to confront, he was ready to take action.

"We'll never get past his security," Paul countered.

Irritation nipped at Zeke. "So are we supposed to do nothing?" he demanded of Paul.

"If we barge in there with accusations,

we'll be booted out, and he'll cover his tracks and come up with alibis."

"If you think he hasn't already come up with his alibi, you don't know politicians very well," Josh stated. "He knows he had a woman killed. He's going to have already covered his tracks for that death."

"Exactly," John said, intervening. "We need to investigate the men he's sent after Kellyanne and Brady. If we can connect them to the senator, we have something to go to the authorities with. We'll have more proof. An affair can be forgiven by the public. Murder can't be."

Kellyanne shuddered and rubbed her arms at the mention of the word *murder.* Zeke knelt beside her chair. "We're not going to let that happen to you or Brady." He reached for her hand, and she gave it willingly even in front of her family.

Josh closed the computer and removed the flash drive. "If you don't mind, I'm going to lock this up inside my safe at my office."

"I think that's a good idea," Zeke said. "They only think we have it. If they knew for certain we do, they'd never stop coming after it." They needed to keep it safe and make a few copies. If Davenport wanted this information kept quiet, there was no telling what else he might do to retrieve it.

"In the meantime, we need to be prepared to leave first thing in the morning. The farther away Kellyanne and Brady are, the safer they'll be."

Josh left with the flash drive, and the rest of the family dispersed, getting back to the business of packing up for their secret sprint to the fishing cabin.

Once there, they wouldn't have access to the outside world aside from the burner cell phones Josh had purchased, which would have spotty reception at best, and a radio Zeke had packed. They needed to bring food and baby supplies and weapons and hunker down until her brothers decided it was safe enough.

He didn't relish the idea of hiding out, but he had one job now, and that was to keep Kellyanne and Brady safe. They were growing more and more important to him every day, despite his attempts to keep his heart guarded.

She might break his heart again once this was over, but for now, she needed him, and he wasn't going to let her down.

* * *

Before dawn the next morning, the truck was loaded up and they were on the road. They'd decided to leave from Zeke's place, so they hauled the horse trailer over there and then saddled the horses and loaded one with supplies. Paul joined Kellyanne and Zeke on another horse to follow them to the cabin so he would know where it was located.

Kellyanne had Brady in a carrier strapped to her as she rode. Zeke led them toward the river and then made a right and headed up a steep hill. When they neared the end of the strong current, he pointed toward an isolated, elevated cabin.

"That's the place."

It didn't look as bad as Kellyanne had expected, but she recalled Zeke saying he'd come by to clean up the place a few months ago. However, she doubted many people had been around. The river, which had had a strong current only a few miles back, was barely trickling here. Whatever water his grandfather had once fished in had been dammed up years ago, leaving only a muddy riverbed with a creek-sized body of water remaining.

Once they reached the cabin, Zeke helped

her climb off the horse, being careful with Brady. She couldn't believe how well he was behaving. During the two-hour ride, he'd glanced around and enjoyed the sunshine, fresh air and nature on display. His blue eyes had been wide with wonder and ever so observant. Now he was growing fussy and hot, and she couldn't blame him. She was exhausted too.

The cabin had been built on stilts when the water was obviously much more of a threat than it was now, but its elevated status added a level of comfort. At least they would be able to see anyone trying to sneak up on them in time. She grabbed Brady's supplies and carried him up the steps to the front door.

While Zeke and Paul carried in the rest of the supplies, Kellyanne unstrapped Brady, changed him and found a sleeping bag for him to lie on while she helped them unpack the supplies. She would have to find a better place for him since they'd had to leave the Pack 'n Play behind for lack of room on the horses.

One of the things they had brought was a radio with a receiver good enough to reach her family to be used only as necessary. As she watched Paul and Zeke set it up and test it, it occurred to her that they might be here for a long time. You didn't get to be in Davenport's position without making powerful friends who would be willing to turn their heads or do his bidding for a price.

She shuddered at the thought of him trying to snatch Brady again. If he didn't want him, he should just leave them alone. She would never tell anyone about Brady's parentage if it kept him safe. She would be just fine letting everyone believe he was her baby. Hers and Zeke's.

She stole a glance at Zeke as that idea turned in her mind. They'd grown closer since that day he'd first arrived at her apartment and taken them both under his protection, and it was obvious he'd grown to care about Brady, but was he ready to take on the responsibilities of raising a child?

And why was she even allowing her thoughts to go down that road? She still owed him the truth about their baby, and that would destroy any chance of a future between them.

When everything was settled, Paul hugged her, said goodbye and left. They watched him climb onto his horse and hurry away. A part of her was sad to see him go, but she wanted her privacy. Now she was getting it.

It didn't take long before they had everything put away. Zeke pulled out an old dresser drawer and cleaned it up to make a bed for Brady. She'd thought about placing him on the bed with pillows surrounding him, but he was just starting to roll, and she was worried he might roll off the bed when she wasn't watching him.

She searched through the cans of food they'd brought before choosing a can of beef stew to heat up for them to eat. Zeke shot her a sorrowful look. "Your brothers will bring more supplies in a few days."

"I don't mind it," she assured him. She wasn't complaining. She felt safe and free here in this secluded cabin with Zeke and Brady.

As the sky outside grew darker, Zeke lit a fire, and they sat before it and ate their makeshift meal. She watched him, in awe of how easily he'd stepped out of his life to keep them safe. He was a good man, the best man she knew.

"How did you get Josh to allow you to come here with me?"

He gave her a curious glance and shrugged. "I just told him I wanted to stay near you and

Brady to keep you both safe. You were there when I did."

"And what would you have done if he'd said no and insisted on coming himself?"

"I don't know. I would have made sure he knew how important it is that I remain with you. I would have insisted on coming."

He would have stood up to her brother. Why couldn't she have that same kind of strength?

"You're very loyal to Josh, aren't you?"

"I like him. He's not like other people in this town. He doesn't hold my past against me."

"Your past? What are you talking about?"

He set down his bowl of stew and leaned back. "I'm the son of a murderer, Kelly. I went to work for a large police department right after leaving the police academy. Someone discovered my father killed my mother, and I had people who looked at me differently. In fact, one attorney even tried to use it to mar my character when I was a witness in court. People in town look at me differently. Even you…" He shrugged and turned back to his food. "Josh never throws that in my face."

Her heart broke to know his father's actions continued to haunt him all these years later, but why had he included her in that list? "I guess I knew about it, but I never saw you differently because of it."

"Didn't you? Isn't that why you never wanted people to know about us, Kelly?"

"I've already told you that was because of my brothers. They tormented my first boyfriend. He still gives me a wide berth to this day if I see him around town." She didn't want to get into a discussion about her brothers. She'd noticed how much he seemed to want Josh's approval. Maybe it was because they both had tragic histories. "You know Josh's wife was murdered. Some people believe he was responsible."

"I've heard the rumors, but I've never looked into it. I have a difficult time believing he could do something like that."

"Oh no, of course, he didn't do it. And you didn't do anything either, Zeke. You're not responsible for your father's acts or what some people might think of you."

"Well, it's defined me for most of my life. It's kept me from going after the things I wanted."

"And what did you want, Zeke?"

He locked eyes with her. "You." Then his face reddened, and he dropped his head. "But then I never could have given you what you deserved, Kelly. I can't even give you a decent place to hide out while you're running for your life. This place is a dump."

She touched his arm and felt how tense he was. He was really upset at having to be here. But she wasn't. "Zeke, I like this cabin. It isn't much, but you've kept us safe. This isn't permanent, and I have to be honest, I wouldn't care if it was, as long as we could be together."

He glanced down at her, and she saw his eyes fall to her lips. She was drawn to him, and he must feel it too.

He pushed away from her and stood and walked to the fireplace, then knelt to stoke the fire. "You don't mean that, Kelly. Don't say it if you don't mean it."

"What are you talking about?"

He turned and locked eyes with her. "I've given you everything I ever had to give, and it was never enough for you. I'd finally gotten over you. I came to see you that night to tell you I was finally over you. But I got pulled back in."

She felt like he'd slapped her, and she wanted to lash out, but the pain on his face stopped her. She'd made him feel unwanted, unloved, like nothing he could do was right. How could she have made him feel just as awful as she did?

Shame filled her. She was a terrible person.

"I understand why you never wanted to be with me. Sure, we had fun, but I don't think you were ever as serious about me as I was about you." He looked at her. "I wanted to marry you, Kelly. I had dreams about starting a family with you and growing old with you."

She caught her breath. She'd never realized he'd been that serious. "You did?"

"But to you, we were nothing but fun and games."

She stood and went to him, pressing her hands onto his chest. "Zeke, I wanted that too."

"But you left. If you'd really wanted to be with me, you should have at least asked me to go with you."

"You had your grandmother to think about. I didn't think you would ever leave her. Besides, I know how much you love this place. I couldn't stay, but it didn't have anything to do with you, Zeke." She touched his cheek and leaned in for a kiss, brushing her lips against his.

When she did, he pulled his arms around

her and dragged her close, and she soaked in the feel of his arms around her. He could have been hers all along, and she hated that she'd ever made him feel inferior. He was everything she'd ever wanted.

When the kiss broke, he rested his forehead against hers and caught his breath. "What about who I am, Kelly? What about your family? I'll never be good enough for you."

"Why do you think anyone would think that?"

He leaned back and pulled a hand through his hair. "Because of who I am. My father killed my mother. I've had to live with that shame. People have judged me for that all my life. What kind of person can I be when I come from such violence?"

She was stunned by his confession. She'd known about his folks and how they died, but she'd honestly thought he'd coped well with the trauma. It certainly had never colored how she'd viewed him. "You're not damaged. You're a good man, better than I deserve."

"No. You deserve everything." He stared into her eyes. "I love you, Kelly. I've always loved you. Every time I watched you leave town and forget about me, I tried to convince myself that I'd fooled myself into believing you loved me too."

She touched his cheek as his words broke her. Her selfishness knew no bounds. "Oh, Zeke, I'm so sorry."

"I'm not looking for an apology. I don't want it. I don't care about that stuff anymore. It doesn't matter to me how many times you push me away. I want to be with you, and I will always be there for you whenever you want me."

Her heart leaped. He was offering her everything she wanted. "I love you too, and I want us to be together." But she couldn't continue to keep this secret from him if they ever hoped to have a future together. "I need to tell you something—"

He placed his finger on her lips to stop her from speaking. "Don't say it. Don't ruin this. Please don't ruin this. Tonight is everything I've ever wanted. We can deal with the rest of it tomorrow."

She leaned into him. He deserved the truth and she only hoped—prayed—he would be able to forgive her once he knew it. But for now, she was enjoying the blessing of being in his arms.

* * *

Three days passed, and Kellyanne, Zeke and Brady spent them quietly, taking walks along the bank of the river, horseback riding, reading and talking in front of a burning fire at night.

Kellyanne loved every moment of it. She would've forgotten that she was in danger if it weren't for Zeke's guarded demeanor and multiple patrols per day. She might have let down her guard, but he hadn't. She still hadn't brought herself to tell him her terrible, terrible secret.

On the third day, she'd just finished feeding Brady his lunch when they heard what sounded like horse hoofs approaching.

Zeke tensed and reached for his rifle as he walked to the door and opened it cautiously. His body relaxed, and he pushed it open. "It's your brother Colby."

Colby? When had he arrived in town and why?

She stepped outside and saw it was indeed Colby approaching on horseback and walking another horse loaded with supplies. Zeke placed the rifle by the door and hurried down to help Colby unload.

He waved, and she waved back and then

took Brady inside to clean him up. She'd known their time alone would be limited. They needed fresh supplies. Plus, she was anxious to hear if her brother had any updates on the situation with Davenport. They'd been leery to use the radio to talk about things that important in case their conversations could be intercepted, but if they'd gotten that matter settled once and for all, she might have this happy little life with Zeke and Brady for good.

Colby entered carrying a box full of food. "Zeke will be up in a minute. He's going to take care of my horses." He set the crate on the counter, turned to Kellyanne and pulled her into a hug.

She soaked in his calming presence. His job as an FBI agent often kept him away from home during the holidays, and Kellyanne realized they hadn't seen one another in well over a year. "I wasn't expecting you. When did you arrive in town?"

"We got in last night."

"We?" Colby was single and didn't have a family, so his use of the plural interested her.

"Miles and I drove up together."

So Josh had called in Colby and Miles, needing some federal backup. She wasn't surprised, given the name of their primary suspect. "Did Melissa and Dylan come too?"

"No, Miles thought it would be best to leave them at home in case there's any threat of danger."

She nodded. Miles was always thinking of his family first. "And did Josh show you the photos?"

"He did."

"And what do you think?"

He pulled a hand through his hair. "This is big, Kelly. Senator Davenport is predicted to win the election in a landslide. People are even saying he'll one day run for president. The man is a powerhouse with friends all over the state and in Washington."

"I know. I couldn't believe it either."

"Why wouldn't your friend tell you about this?"

"I guess she wanted to protect him. She thought he loved her, but when she discovered he was having affairs with other women, too, she changed her mind." He gave her a stare that made her uncomfortable. As the second oldest of her brothers, Colby had a presence that served him well in the FBI. He turned that look on her now, and she didn't care for it. "You're acting like I was the one who had the affair with a married, prominent politician. It wasn't me."

"But she was your friend, right?" His tone implied she shouldn't have associated with someone who would do such a thing.

She bit her lip to hold back her anger at having one of her brothers question her decision-making. She didn't want to lash out as she'd done in the past so she decided to take the same approach Zeke did, calm and composed. "Why do you do that?" she asked Colby. "Why must you question every decision I make as if I'm not capable of living my own life?"

He looked like he was going to refute her claim, but then his expression twisted, and he scrubbed a hand over his chin. "I just did that, didn't I?"

"Yes, you did. It's not just you, Colby. I love all my brothers, but you all never give me a chance to prove that I'm not a little girl anymore."

He sat down on the hearth and rubbed his hands together. "You're right. We do treat you that way sometimes." He glanced at her and then shrugged. "All right, all the time. But we're your brothers. It's our job to protect you and help you, but I suppose we do sometimes swerve into being controlling and over-protective."

"I know that you care about me, Colby, and I appreciate that you want to keep me safe, but I'd also like to feel free to make my own choices without being judged for them. I'm not the only one who makes mistakes."

"No, you're definitely not the only one." Pain flickered through his eyes, leaving Kellyanne to wonder if he was referring to something specific in his life. It meant a lot to her that he could admit he and the rest of her brothers had been controlling and overbearing at times, but it also felt good to stand up for herself and actually have him listen to her and acknowledge her feelings.

"Lisa was a good person, Colby. She made a mistake, but once she had Brady, all she cared about was giving him a good life."

"Brady? That's her baby, right?"

"That's right."

He stood and leaned against the mantel, his head lowered. He glanced at Brady on a pallet on the floor and then looked back at Kellyanne. Confusion muddled his expression now. "This is your friend's baby?"

"That's right. His name is Brady." She was tired of the questioning looks. "What is the

matter with you, Colby? Why are you behaving this way? Yes, she had an affair with
a married man. Yes, she got pregnant without being married. I know it's not the way it
should have been, but it's not the end of the
world. You act like you're accusing me instead of her."

"No, I'm only trying to get to the truth of
the matter, Kelly, and I don't believe you're
being totally honest with me, with anyone.
That's why I told Josh I wanted to be the one
to come here today. I need to sort out the
truth."

"What are you talking about?"

He gave an exasperated sigh. "If this is
your friend's baby…" He locked eyes with
her before he continued. "Where is your baby,
Kelly? What happened to it?"

She gasped and felt all the air leave her
body. She fell onto the couch. "What? How
did—" She tried to laugh at the absurdity. He
couldn't possibly know. He couldn't. "I don't
have a baby."

He sat on the coffee table and pierced her
with his gaze. "I was in Austin months ago
on an assignment. It wrapped up quickly and
unexpectedly, so I thought I would drop by
your apartment and take you to dinner."

Tears pressed against her eyes. She saw it in his face. He knew.

She tried to pull her hands away, but he held them tightly. "I knocked on your door, but you didn't answer, then I saw you as I was headed back to my car. You were walking by the lake with another woman. I started to approach you, but then I saw… I didn't want to put you on the spot, so I left before either of you saw me, fully expecting to receive a phone call in a few months telling me that you'd had a baby. That call never came."

She pulled her hands away and stood. "I don't know what you think you saw, Colby, but—"

"I know what I heard too, Kelly. You were talking about being pregnant. I heard you. You were obviously pregnant and now you show up here with a baby you claim isn't yours and someone chasing you. If Brady isn't yours, then I have to ask, what happened to your baby?"

A noise behind her grabbed her attention. She spun around and saw Zeke standing in the doorway. He'd obviously been carrying firewood, because it now piled at his feet. His face was gray, and his eyes were wide with shock.

Her worst fear had been realized. He'd heard Colby's question.

Zeke approached her. "You were pregnant?" It was an accusation more than a question.

She stumbled over her words, wishing she could shoot daggers into Colby and his big mouth. This was not how she wanted Zeke to find out, but now there was no choice but to come clean. "I—I was pregnant. Colby's right. He wasn't imagining it."

Zeke rubbed his face. "Who was the father, Kelly?"

She glared at him. "Who do you think? It was you. It's always only been you."

He spun around and paced the floor, his hands flailing around uncertainly. Finally, he turned back, zeroing in on her. "Then what happened to *our* child? Where is he? Did you get rid of him without telling me?"

"No!" She was shocked he would even ask that question. She would have hoped he'd thought more of her than that. "I had every intention of telling you, Zeke. I was looking forward to telling you and to being a mom."

"Then what happened?"

"I lost the baby. I miscarried. I was getting ready to tell you that you were going to be a father." She took a breath, and the pain of her loss hit her again. "And then you weren't a father anymore, and I didn't know what to do. How could I tell you that you were almost a father? I'm sorry. I wanted you to know, but I didn't want you to think I was so reckless that I couldn't even take care of our baby."

Colby's eyes narrowed, changing from suspicion to understanding. "You didn't choose it, Kellyanne. You didn't do anything wrong."

She appreciated her brother saying so, but it wasn't really his opinion she wanted to hear. Zeke still hadn't responded, and the look on his face still held shock and disgust.

"I couldn't take care of our child, and now I can't take care of Brady. I'm a failure as a mother."

Colby tried to intervene again. "Kelly—"

"No, you're not," Zeke finally stated. "You've taken great care of Brady, and I know you'll make a great mom one day to your own child."

She looked up into his face. "But not to our child, right?" All her hopes and dreams were fading away right in front of her.

He looked at her, his eyes sorrowful. "You should have told me, Kelly. I could have been there for you. You should have allowed me to go through this with you. Instead, you denied me my right to know I had fathered a child."

"I'm sorry, Zeke. I was just so ashamed. I should have taken better care of myself. This might not have happened."

"And it might still have happened. I find it hard to believe you had any control over that. I don't blame you for miscarrying our baby." His jaw tightened before he continued. "But I do blame you for keeping it from me."

She'd known this was coming, but she'd fallen in love with Zeke anyway. She wanted to make a life with him, and now that her shame had been revealed, he didn't want her.

"I'm sorry."

Zeke pushed his hands through his hair and paced the room, his agitation growing. "I shouldn't be surprised. Why am I surprised? I thought you had changed, Kelly. I thought you had grown, but you're still the same selfish woman I've always known. You didn't tell me because you needed me to be here with you. You kept this from me so I wouldn't leave. That doesn't sound like someone who's grown."

"Please, Zeke, I didn't mean to hurt you. I tried to tell you several times. I wanted you to know."

He spun to face her. "But not enough to pick up the phone and call me."

Irritation bit through her. She'd apologized, but he wouldn't listen to reason. "I was upset, Zeke. Can't you understand that? I lost something precious. A baby I wanted so much. I was devastated. I was a mess. What could you have done if you'd known? How could you have changed that?"

"I could have been there for you." He spat the words at her, his anger and indignation taking over. "I could have comforted you and grieved with you. You denied me that. Your selfishness denied me everything."

His answer stunned her. She had expected him to be angry, but she'd thought he might at least listen to her. She couldn't go backward in time and make a different decision. She'd apologized. There wasn't anything more she could do.

"I'm sorry I hurt you," she whispered. She picked up her hat and jacket and walked down the steps.

Zeke followed her. "What are you doing? Where are you going?"

"I need a break, Zeke. I'm taking a ride." She grabbed the rein of one of the horses and climbed into the saddle.

"You're running away. Again." His tone had a bite in it that stung her. Tears pressed against her eyes. He was right, but she needed to get away from him before she did or said something she would regret.

She turned the horse and took off, leaving him there. She knew he wouldn't come after her, not with Brady still inside. He would stay and protect him even if it meant watching her ride away. She was relying on his decency to let her go.

Zeke stomped back up the steps into the cabin and slammed the door hard, causing Brady to startle and start to cry. Colby walked over and spoke to the baby, settling him down.

Shame filled Zeke for his hasty action. He hadn't meant to scare Brady. Kelly just made him so mad sometimes, and seeing her once again run away from her problems left a bitter taste in his mouth.

He'd thought he meant something to her, but then how could she have kept this from him?

"I'm sorry I said anything," Colby stated, picking up Brady and rocking him against his shoulder to settle him.

"It's not your fault," Zeke said, although he did wish Colby had never come, or that he'd walked back to the cabin minutes later and never heard the terrible truth, never learned the secret Kellyanne had kept from him.

"I'll watch the baby if you want to go talk to her?"

They did need to talk, but he wasn't sure he was up to it. Seeing her leave had reopened that wound inside of him that reminded him he wasn't good enough. He shook his head and took Brady from Colby. "She'll be back."

He knew she might leave him, but she wouldn't run away without taking Brady. She loved this little fella too much.

Colby picked up his hat. "I'll go make sure she's all right."

Zeke nodded and watched Colby walk away. When he was gone, Zeke fell to his knees.

God, what am I supposed to do with this information?

He'd been ready for a family for so long, and learning that Kelly had been pregnant and lost the baby hurt him. She'd had months to process it, and months to tell him, yet she'd chosen not to.

Brady began to cry, so Zeke got up and

placed him back onto his stomach on the blanket and arranged a few toys for him to play with as he tried to figure out what he was going to do.

He couldn't abandon Kellyanne and Brady. That wasn't even an option. He'd made a promise to keep them safe and protected, and he intended to keep it. But how were they supposed to continue staying in this cabin alone together after what he'd just learned? And how could he ever truly forgive her for what she'd stolen from him?

He'd learned through studying the Bible that forgiveness was a choice, not a feeling. He thought he'd forgiven his father for his actions and put that anger behind him, but now it was rolling back and smothering him in the guise of yet another betrayal by someone he loved. He tried to shake off the feeling that this was all he deserved. He knew that was not true. Jesus had died for him. No matter how much pain Kelly had caused his heart, that didn't compare to the sacrifice Jesus had made for him.

He had to forgive her, and he would. Of course, he would. He loved her. As much as he tried to fight it, he loved her and knew he would eventually forgive her for anything.

He heard footsteps on the porch and figured either she'd returned or Colby had. He sighed. He still didn't know what he was going to say to her. So many angry words pressed against his lips, and he pushed them back. He wanted to have a rational conversation, and anger would derail that and send her on the defensive again. He needed her to stay, and that meant he had to have the cooler head.

He turned as the door opened, but it wasn't Kellyanne or Colby. Thomas Stanford, the man who'd set the fire at the ranch and tried to kidnap Brady, stood in the doorway, and another man stood behind him.

Zeke eyed the rifle by the door. He'd never be able to reach it, but that didn't mean he wouldn't fight.

The men ran at him, grabbing him around the neck and pulling him to the ground. Zeke fought back as Stanford and the other man slammed his head against the counter. Stars appeared in his vision, and his ears rang, but he jabbed Stanford with his elbow and sent the man falling backward. Brady cried at the commotion, but Zeke couldn't take the time to comfort him. The other man grabbed Zeke from behind and pulled him to the ground before picking up a pan from the stove and slamming it against Zeke's head.

Pain burst through him, and the spots in his eyes returned then faded. Everything started to fade. He was losing consciousness fast.

His head felt like deadweight, but Zeke managed to look up at Stanford, who was wiping blood from his nose. "Grab the kid," Stanford told his accomplice, who hurried over and picked up the crying baby.

No!

He tried to yell, but nothing came out. The men left the cabin, the sound of Brady's cries mingling with their boots on the hard steps. He tried to pull himself up but couldn't move.

God, please help me.

The room turned over and over, sending him into a dizzying spin as darkness pulled him under.

EIGHT

Kellyanne pushed the horse into a gallop along the riverbank as tears fell from her face. Rain began to mirror her mood. Finally, she stopped close by the river and jumped off.

She'd destroyed everything. She'd lost Zeke for good. She didn't deserve to be Brady's mother. She didn't deserve Zeke or his love.

Why did she always mess everything up? Everything she tried to do ended in disaster. She'd tried hard to make a life for herself in Austin away from the ranch, away from her family, but it had all fallen apart.

She pushed tears away and watched the water flowing down the river. It never stopped running and that irritated her. Life, it never gave up. It just kept going.

She knew all the consequences of her choices were her own fault. She should have tried to live more as her parents wanted, the

Christian way of life. She'd rebelled because she didn't want to follow a God who made decisions for her like her brothers did. She knew they meant well and only wanted what was best for her, and a realization dawned on her.

God wanted what was best for her.

Maybe He wasn't trying to control her. Maybe He was trying to protect her. Her family and Zeke had rules, rules she didn't like but that she was following because they were meant to protect her and Brady and keep them safe.

She certainly had made too many mistakes on her own by ignoring God's ways. She'd done life her way, and it wasn't good. She wasn't happy. But Zeke had found God, he'd decided to follow Jesus, and she could see the change in him. He had a peace about him that she envied.

She was so tired of fighting, so tired of the drudgery. So tired of blaming herself for everything that went wrong. Lisa's death wasn't her fault. The miscarriage wasn't her fault. She hadn't placed Brady in harm's way. In her haste to keep her family from trying to rule her life, she'd missed out on them being there for her.

She knelt beside the river and tossed in a branch.

But would God give her a second chance? Did He still want her even after all she'd done and how much she'd messed up?

A verse in Romans came back to her. Something about there being no condemnation for people who loved Jesus and accepted Him as savior. She liked the idea of that. Someone who would look at all she'd done and not condemn her.

It was what she wished for from Zeke, but she knew he would never forgive her after what she'd done. Maybe the miscarriage hadn't been her fault, but keeping it from him had been. She should have called him and told him, but she'd been so wrapped up in her own grief and selfishness that she hadn't thought about him and how he would feel.

She was selfish. She'd been selfish and childish, and it was time she grew up and accepted that she didn't know everything, and just because she could make her own choices didn't mean she shouldn't sometimes listen to other people's opinions, like her family's.

She stood and wiped away tears. She was tired of the fighting and pushing away people who loved her. She wanted to be better, wanted to be an example for Brady. But she couldn't do it alone. She couldn't make herself into a better person.

God, I need You. I know You sent Your Son to give me a new life. I want that life. I surrender everything to You, Jesus.

From now on, her life would be about other people instead of herself.

It wouldn't be easy, but she already felt better.

"I thought I heard someone out here."

She spun around at the voice behind her. Thomas Stanford, the man who'd attacked them at the house, stood only a few feet away.

Her heart pounded against her chest, and she backed away. Blood covered his face, and his nose looked swollen, indicating a recent struggle. Panic gripped her. Had he already been to the cabin? Zeke? Brady? Were they okay? They couldn't be if Stanford was out here looking like that.

She glanced at his hand and saw he was holding a rifle, one she recognized. It was Zeke's.

Oh, God, please let them be safe.

"Where did you get that?" she demanded, pointing at the rifle.

He glanced at it and laughed. "From your

boyfriend, of course." He grabbed her arm and dragged her toward him. "You're coming with me too. The boss wants both you and the kid taken care of."

Brady! He has Brady!

She determined then that she wasn't going to fight him. She had to get to Brady and make sure they didn't hurt him.

But her brother had another idea. She spotted Colby in the brush, gun raised at Stanford's head. She tried to warn him off, but he fired before she could even capture his attention.

Stanford ducked at the sound and shoved her to the ground. He picked up the rifle, returned fire and then darted into the trees. Colby chased after him for several minutes and fired twice more before returning to her and helping her up.

"Are you okay?"

"Colby, where's Zeke?"

"I left him back at the cabin. Why?"

"That man, Stanford, he said he has Brady."

Colby's jaw tightened. "I didn't see anyone else out here besides him. He must have been lying so you'd go with him more willingly."

That made sense, but she had a sudden, desperate need to make certain. "We have to go back to the cabin. I think Stanford has Zeke's rifle."

He nodded, helped her mount her horse, then climbed into his saddle, and they headed back the way she'd come.

She'd been foolish to run away, and all she could think about was getting back to Zeke and Brady. She didn't know what she would do if she lost either of them.

She pulled the horse to a stop at the cabin and slid off, but something grabbed her attention before she ran outside. On the ground, just feet away, lay a tiny cowboy boot, the same one Brady had been wearing earlier when she'd left him.

She picked it up and swallowed hard. Colby touched her shoulder, and she knew he was thinking the same thing she was. If Brady's boot was here, Stanford must have taken him. He wouldn't have been able to do that without Zeke putting up a fight.

She turned and ran up the steps. The front door stood open, and the first thing she saw was Zeke sprawled unconscious on the floor. She ran to him, tears pouring down her face, and they didn't stop when she realized he was still breathing.

Colby followed her inside and grabbed a

wet towel to stop the bleeding from a gash on his head. Kellyanne rushed to check on Brady, but the blanket was empty. She checked the bedroom, but he was gone. Stanford had taken Brady just as he'd claimed.

Zeke had been hurt and Brady was gone. She fell to her knees and sobbed.

They were nearly back to Zeke's ranch before his ears stopped ringing from the blow to the head Stanford had given him. He'd awoken to Kellyanne's sobbing, and that sound would haunt him for the rest of his life.

They'd abandoned the supplies at the cabin, mounted their horses and headed home, with Colby alerting their brothers to what had happened on the radio. By the time they reached the ranch, Josh had an ambulance waiting to check Zeke out.

"I've issued an Amber Alert for Brady and locked down the county. If anyone spots Stanford, he won't get away."

But Zeke knew he was probably long gone by now. "There were two of them. Stanford had someone with him. He was younger, taller with blond hair."

"He must have gone ahead with the baby while Stanford went after Kelly."

"But how did they know where we were?" Kellyanne asked. "How did they find us?"

Josh shook his head. "That's a good question. Maybe they had people staking us out or followed the radio signal."

Colby rubbed his face. "Or they followed me there. I had to have led them right to you. I'm sorry, Kelly. I had no idea I was being followed."

She hugged her brother to let him know she didn't blame him. She was devastated but hadn't turned to blaming anyone. Zeke was glad about that, sure he would be on the top of that list. He should never have allowed his anger at her to distract him.

"If they followed you, they were definitely watching either us or Zeke's place, otherwise they wouldn't have known to follow you. I doubt that fella with Stanford was the only one he was working with. My guess is Davenport has put out a team of people looking for Kelly and Brady."

"And now they have Brady," she whispered.

Zeke stood and pulled her to him, and she went willingly into his arms. Nothing else mattered now except finding Brady and bringing him home safely, and Zeke was determined to do just that.

Kellyanne sat on the bench outside the bullpen at the sheriff's office. She leaned forward and put her hands over her face.

Brady was gone. Her baby was gone.

Tears pressed against her eyes, but she refused to cry. This was her fault. Brady was in danger because of her.

God, why are You punishing him for my mistakes?

Zeke approached her and slid onto the bench beside her. She couldn't deal with him either. He had to blame her. He had to blame her for yet another mess she'd made. Yet when he reached for her hand and held it, she didn't feel any condemnation.

She dared a look into his eyes and saw sympathy and understanding there instead of accusations.

"He's going to be okay," he assured her. "We're going to find him."

Yes, they knew who had taken him, who had arranged for it to happen. Senator Davenport. A force of nature in the political world. He wouldn't have gotten his hands dirty. He had someone else do his deeds.

"He's Brady's father. He could easily have a judge in his pocket who will say we have no right to have him, and that he just took Brady because he belongs to him."

Zeke held her hand. "He'd have to claim him to do that, and that's the last thing he wants to do. He wants to keep Brady a secret, remember?"

"There's no telling what he'll do with him." All the terrible things that could happen to a small child rushed through her mind and made her stomach turn. What were they planning to do to a four-month-old who couldn't even protect himself? What kind of a monster would hurt a child?

"Kelly, we still have what he wants, remember? The flash drive."

Suddenly, she realized what he was implying. "You think he'll use Brady to try to get it?"

"I think it's probable he'll try to trade Brady for it. After all, as long as we have that flash drive, we control him."

She shook her head. It didn't feel like they were in control of anything. "What do we do now?"

"There's not much we can do except wait. We're going to meet with your brothers in a few minutes. We're going to try to figure out a strategy. Don't worry. Getting Brady back is our primary concern."

"Zeke, let him have the flash drive. I don't care. Let him get away with it. All I care about is getting Brady back. All I care about is bringing him back home."

He nodded, leaned over and kissed her cheek before heading toward the glassed-in conference room.

She froze, panic creeping up her neck. She couldn't sit and listen to them brainstorm options for finding her child without falling apart. She just couldn't do it.

Zeke turned back to her. "Aren't you coming?"

She stared at her brothers, already in the conference room. She was grateful to have them on her side. What a fool she'd been before for taking them for granted.

She looked up at him as tears pressed against her eyes. "I don't think I can."

His expression softened and she knew he understood. "Are you sure?"

She nodded. "I trust you...all of you."

He gave her hand a squeeze then walked into the conference room to join her brothers.

Zeke's anger seemed to have dissipated.

Was he finally on his way to forgiving her? But did it even matter now? She would never survive losing two children. He'd come to love Brady as much as she did, and she'd even started to think about being a family with them. That would never happen.

All she cared about now was bringing Brady home.

Her phone beeped, and she reached for it. Her eyes widened, and her heart stopped at the image on the text message. It was a photo of Brady along with a newspaper dated today and the words Bring the flash drive if you want to see him again. Will tell you where to go once you're on the way.

She gasped and stood. Zeke needed to see this. Maybe they could trace the message back to the caller. She hurried toward the conference room but stopped before reaching for the door as her phone dinged another message.

Come alone. No cops or the kid dies.

Her heart sank into her stomach. There was no telling what they would do to Brady if she didn't follow their instructions exactly. Zeke would be busy with her brothers long enough for her to retrieve the flash drive and leave.

She walked to Josh's office quickly and closed the door behind her. She knew he'd placed the flash drive in his safe in his office, but she also knew from past experience that the combination was his late wife's birth date. She'd noticed previously how he hitched each time he used it and figured it out by watching him.

She took a breath, hoping he hadn't changed it in the last year. She spun the dial to the combination and held her breath until she pulled on the knob and the safe opened. She reached in and retrieved the flash drive. A sinking feeling filled her. Her instincts were competing. Part of her wanted to march back into the conference room and tell Zeke and her brothers about the mystery text and demand. The other part of her wanted to do everything she could to make certain Brady was safe, and that meant doing whatever the kidnappers demanded.

She slipped the flash drive into her pocket, closed the safe, then dug the spare key from Zeke's desk where she knew he kept it. She walked out and got into Zeke's truck and was two miles down the road before she breathed a sigh of relief that she'd actually gotten away with the flash drive.

She pulled over and took out her phone. She responded to the text.

I've got the flash drive. Where can we meet?

Where are you?

Two miles from the sheriff's station. Hwy 17. Keep driving. Someone will find you.

She placed the phone on the seat beside her. This was it. This was her decision. There was still time to turn back, and she did want to. There was a good chance the kidnappers would double-cross her and take the flash drive and still kill them both. She could phone Zeke right now and tell him what she'd done, and he would come to rescue her, but that would mean Brady would be in more danger. No, she'd made her decision. There was no turning back now.

She put the truck into gear and drove. Several minutes later, a car approached her from behind. She gripped the steering wheel as fear rustled through her. The car sped up and passed her but pulled over in front of her, indicating she should do the same. She did so and cut the engine.

Two men exited the vehicle and approached her with guns drawn. "Where is it?" one of them demanded.

She could hand it over to them, but she had no assurance that Brady would be returned if she did. She had to play this smart. "Where's Brady?"

"Give us the flash drive if you want to see him."

"No. First, take me to him. Then you get the flash drive."

One of them grabbed her arm and yanked her from the truck. She dropped the keys in her hand and heard something crack as she was yanked out. She turned and saw her cell phone had fallen out and the screen was damaged.

The man who'd pulled her out patted her down, hitting on the drive in her pocket. He retrieved it and held it to his partner. "Got it."

"You have what you wanted. Now, where is Brady? What has Davenport done to him?"

Her worst fear was that now that they had the flash drive, they would leave, and she would never get Brady back. But that didn't happen. One of them grabbed her arm and pulled her toward the car, but instead of taking her to the back seat, they popped open the trunk.

She stopped and dragged her feet. She wasn't going in there. "No, wait, we had a deal."

The other man tore off a length of duct tape, taped up her hands and mouth, then shoved her inside the trunk of the car and slammed the lid. Darkness enveloped her, and fear spread through her. What had she done? She'd only put herself and Brady in even more danger with no way out of this situation.

Tears pressed against her eyes. She still didn't even know where Brady was or where they were taking her.

I've messed up again.

Her heart shattered. She'd betrayed Zeke and her brothers. She'd walked into a trap, and she was no closer to finding Brady and bringing him home. Her choices might prove fatal for both her and Brady.

Zeke glanced up from his conversation with Kellyanne's brothers and looked to the bench where he'd left her earlier. She wasn't there and that gave him a bad feeling. She'd been on the edge of breaking down before. She didn't need to be alone.

He excused himself and walked out to find her, scanning the bullpen. He checked the breakroom and the offices and didn't see her. His gut clenched and that bad feeling grew.

He pulled out his phone, doubled-checked that he hadn't missed a call or text from her explaining where she was, then hit the button to call her. It rang several times before going to voice mail. He ended the call and shot her a text, then waited as long as he could stand—probably only a few minutes—before texting her again. When there was still no response, he slid into panic mode. Where was she and why wasn't she answering her phone?

He walked to the front desk clerk. "Have you seen Kelly?"

"She left earlier in your truck."

Shock punched him in the gut. "She did *what*?"

He hurried to the door and pulled it open. His truck was gone. He went to his desk and opened his drawer. His spare set of keys was gone. Hopefully she was only headed home, but he had to know for certain. He pulled up the GPS on his truck. It was sitting still on Highway 17.

He called Kellyanne's cell phone again, and when she still didn't answer, he grabbed his jacket. "Go tell Josh his sister left. I'm going after her," he called to the desk clerk. He headed out the door and slid into one of the patrol cruisers.

His gut was telling him something was wrong. Why had Kellyanne left and why was she sitting in his truck on the side of the road and not answering her calls? He tried not to panic, but his mind was already going through all the things that could have gone wrong, including that Davenport's men had grabbed her.

He saw his truck and pulled to the side of the road, parking behind it. The driver's door was standing open, and as he approached the truck, he noticed the engine wasn't running. He knelt and spotted her cell phone and the keys on the ground by the driver's door. That couldn't be good. He scanned the area, hoping to see her out in the field or walking down the shoulder, but there was no sign of her.

He walked the shoulder and noted tire tracks in front of where the truck was parked. Another car had been here and picked her up. The question was did she go willingly or was she taken?

His heart sank, and he wanted to rail against the men who'd done this, but his focus had to be on finding Kelly and Brady. He pulled out his cell phone and called Josh. "I found my truck," he told Josh when he answered. "Kellyanne's gone."

NINE

He couldn't lose her. Not now when he'd finally come to terms with everything that had happened with them. When he'd finally found himself hopeful he could make a life with her and Brady.

He knew she'd never intended to hurt him. Why had she shut him out again now? No, he couldn't allow his thoughts to go there. She must have her reasons. She wouldn't have ditched the truck. She'd been taken, but why? They already had Brady to use as leverage to get the flash drive returned to them.

Her brothers watched him as he paced. He felt their eyes watching him, judging him. He'd promised to keep her safe, and he'd failed to do so.

"This is not just on you," Colby told him.

"I should have kept a better eye on her. Should've had someone with her."

Josh stood and grabbed his shoulder. "We all know that whenever Kelly gets it in her head to do something, there's little anyone can do to stop it. Trust us. We've all tried."

Josh shook his head. "It doesn't make any sense. We haven't received any demands since they abducted Brady. Why not at least make the demand first before taking her."

Zeke recalled the feeling that something was wrong earlier, and a terrible thought occurred to him. She would do anything to make sure Brady was safe. Was it possible she'd gotten a demand? "Unless…" He glanced at the safe where they'd stored the flash drive. He didn't want to believe she'd do something like that without telling anyone but…

Josh followed his gaze. His face hardened, and he walked to the safe, put in the combination and opened the door. His shoulders sagged. "It's gone. The flash drive isn't here."

"How can it be gone?" Colby demanded.

"Kelly took it." Zeke didn't even have to wonder. "She must have gotten a demand from the kidnappers. She wouldn't have risked Brady's life."

"You mean she didn't trust us enough to rescue him." Colby's tone was angry. Zeke didn't blame him, because he was right. Once again, she hadn't trusted anyone, including him. She'd gone off on her own and made a mess of everything. Now, instead of one person to rescue, they had two.

"They had to know we could have easily made a copy of the flash drive." Miles glanced at them. "We did make a copy, didn't we?"

"I had my techs try, but it was encrypted, and I thought that copy was safe."

Zeke's emotions ranged from feeling sick to his stomach, to fighting the urge to punch something. Why would Kellyanne act so rashly? Why hadn't she come to him for help? Once again, she hadn't trusted him.

"Don't take it so personally," Josh insisted, pulling up his chair and taking a seat. "She's known us a lot longer and didn't trust us either."

He looked and saw them all staring at him.

Colby grinned. "You love her." It wasn't a question but a statement, but Zeke felt the need to respond.

"For a long time." He glanced at each of her brothers. "She wanted to keep it a secret because…"

"Because of us," Colby finished. "Apparently, we're overbearing and can't be trusted not to run off any guy who looks at her." He shrugged. "Hey, isn't that what older brothers are for?"

Zeke looked at each one of them. "You're not upset."

"Why would we be?" Josh shot him a stern look. "You're a good man, Zeke. You've proven that time and again, both with your exemplary work as a deputy and with how you've stayed by Kellyanne's side throughout all of this."

"I thought you all might not approve given my background and what happened to my parents."

"We all have skeletons," Josh said. "I wouldn't have let you become part of my team if I thought you weren't a good man."

"What happened to you happened when you were a child. Why would anyone hold that against you?" Lawson asked him.

"I don't know. It just seems like all my life I've been the kid whose father killed his mother. It's defined me."

"It doesn't have to," Colby told him. "You don't have to let it."

"You could have let it define you even more," Josh continued. "You chose to be a good man, Zeke. You chose to make the right choices. You can't blame yourself for what your folks did. None of us can. At some point, everyone has to make their own choices, and you've chosen well."

He took a deep breath. "Good. I'm glad to hear you all say that, because once we get Kelly and Brady back, I want you all to know that I'm not letting them out of my sight again. I want to marry her and give Brady more brothers and sisters. And I'll do whatever it takes to make that happen, even if it means we have to leave Courtland."

Josh nodded, stood and reached out his hand to Zeke. "I believe you will. And if my baby sister ends up leaving Courtland again, I'll be glad to know she's got you looking out for her."

The others added their agreement, and Zeke was glad to have their support. He shook Josh's hand. He didn't want to leave Courtland, but he would do anything and go anywhere to be with her. Nothing else was more important to him than getting her back safely and making her his wife.

"We have to find her and bring her home," Colby stated, echoing his thoughts. "And we still have no idea who Davenport has working for him."

This was all about Davenport. He was the mastermind behind all of this. He'd committed murder and had now abducted Kelly and Brady, all to protect his false political reputation as a man of family values. "I suggest we not worry about the people he's hired. We know who's behind all of this. I say it's time we confront the man himself."

Josh nodded. "I agree. Let's go confront him."

Zeke felt better having a mission. Davenport would tell them where Kelly and Brady had been taken. He would make certain of it. It was all he had left. He climbed into Colby's SUV and psyched himself up for what was to come. He wasn't returning to Courtland without his family.

Kellyanne's heart hammered against her chest as the car finally stopped after what seemed like forever. She heard doors opening and felt the weight of the car shift as the men exited. The trunk opened and the same men hovered over her, then reached inside and grabbed her arm.

"Let's go. Get out."

This was it. She was finally going to confront Davenport and look into the eyes of the man who'd murdered her friend and kidnapped Brady. She prayed he was safe. She also prayed Zeke had realized what had happened and was looking for her.

The men pulled her from a garage into an empty house. Through the uncovered windows, she saw houses that looked abandoned, empty streets and sidewalks. No one was around to hear her if she cried out, and she suspected that was Davenport's plan.

"Keep moving," one of the men said, shoving her through the kitchen and toward the back of the house where they rapped on a door and someone yelled out, "Come in."

They opened the door and pushed her inside. Another man stood by the window in the back bedroom.

"She's here, boss," one of her captors said.

He turned to look at her, and although she did know the man, it wasn't Senator Davenport who stood before her. Instead, it was the man she'd seen Lisa arguing with at the fundraiser.

"Who are you?" she demanded. "Where is Davenport?"

"Senator Davenport knows nothing about

this," he told her. "My name is Ethan Lloyd. I'm Senator Davenport's campaign manager."

"You're the one Lisa confronted at the party."

"That's true. She said she was going to bring him down. I couldn't allow that. It's my job to protect him, even from himself." He turned to look at the men. "Did you bring it?" One of the men handed him the flash drive. He stared at it and then glanced back at Kellyanne. "Thanks for bringing this, by the way. This could have ruined everything we've worked for."

"Why do you want to work for the man who killed Lisa?"

His eyes widened and then he laughed. "Killed Lisa? No, no, no. He didn't kill anyone."

"I know she went to confront him the day she died."

"She didn't get past me. I told you, it's my job to protect Davenport. I made sure she understood no one was going to blackmail us. When she told me about the evidence she had, I had to get it."

"So you killed her?"

His eyes darkened. "She might have lived if she'd only told me where it was. She said she'd hidden it and I would never find it. Once we figured out where the kid was, I figured you must have it. Turns out, I was right. You did." He placed the flash drive onto the windowsill, picked up a hammer and smashed it to bits. He turned back to her and a smug grin spread across his face. "Problem solved."

"You have what you wanted, now where's the baby? Have you hurt him?"

He pointed to the doorway behind him. "He's in there."

The men released her, and she hurried into what looked like a storage room. Brady was lying inside a blue plastic crate. His eyes were red and full of tears, but he appeared unharmed. Relief flooded through her as she reached down and stroked his cheek. She'd done it. *Thank You, God, for keeping him safe.*

She wasn't going to let him out of her sight again. "Everything's going to be okay now," she promised, but, as she glanced up and saw Ethan watching her with his cold, calculating stare, a sickening feeling settled in the pit of her stomach.

Returning the flash drive wasn't going to be enough to save them. Brady's mere existence was proof of the affair, and Ethan had confessed to Kellyanne.

He motioned to one of the men who approached Kellyanne. She backed away from him, afraid of what he was going to do. She spotted the crowbar in his hand moments before he slammed it against her head.

Pain riddled through her, and she fell to the floor as the man walked out, closed the door behind him and locked it. Brady's cries were the last thing she heard before she lost consciousness.

Josh pulled the SUV to a curb in front of the television station. Colby had managed to call the senator's office and get a copy of his schedule, which included a live broadcast from the television station in Dallas. It was the perfect opportunity to ambush him and Zeke was glad they didn't have to lose time making the drive to Austin. Dallas was much closer, and time was running out for Kelly and Brady.

Colby flashed his FBI credentials at the front desk. The receptionist asked them to wait, but Zeke wasn't going to give Davenport's security team time to react. He pushed past them and left the brothers to deal with them.

He found the studio where the interview was taking place and forced his way inside, hurrying past the cameras to the platform where Davenport sat talking with a reporter.

The reporter saw him first and stood. "Who are you? What do you want?"

Davenport turned just as Zeke reached him.

"Where are they," he demanded of Davenport.

The man stood and faced him. "Excuse me?"

"Where are Kellyanne and Brady?"

"I don't know who those people are." He looked past Zeke to his security team, but Zeke pushed him back into his seat.

"They can't help you right now. Tell me where Kellyanne and Brady are."

"I've already told you, I don't know who you're looking for. Why do you believe I do?"

"Because Brady is your child and you've done everything in your power to keep his identity from coming out."

He stared at Zeke, his eyes widened and his mouth parted. "What—what do you mean, he's my child? What nonsense is this? Who do you work for? The opposition?"

Zeke wasn't going to let this man talk his

way out of this. "Lisa Adams was his mother. She was murdered last week, and since then, you've done everything in your power to prevent news of the affair from coming out."

Davenport glanced around, and only then did Zeke realize the cameras were still rolling. He spotted someone announcing they were broadcasting live. Davenport's affair was no longer secret.

He must have realized it, too, because his shoulders stiffened, and he straightened his tie. "I can assure you, I have no idea what you're talking about."

"A woman and a four-month-old child are missing, Senator. What are you going to do about it?"

He grabbed Zeke's arm and pulled him from the stage as several people, obviously his aides, rushed to the stage and demanded the cameras be turned off.

Only once they were out of camera range did Davenport turn to him. By that time, Josh, Miles, Lawson, Paul and Colby had joined them. "You said Lisa Adams was killed?"

"Murdered in her home after she said she was going to confront you."

"Look, I don't know who you are—"

Zeke held out his deputy sheriff's badge,

and Kellyanne's brothers flashed their credentials, as well. Senator Davenport focused in on Colby's, and he paled. "I never saw Lisa after she ended things with me. She never came to see me."

"And the baby?"

"I knew she'd gotten pregnant, but she said she was going to get rid of it. She ended the affair with me, and I haven't seen or heard another word from her."

"Really? It seems coincidental that she was going to confront you and then wound up dead. Talk about a scandal."

Davenport held up his hands. "Now wait a minute. I didn't kill anyone, and I didn't abduct anyone either. I have no idea who this woman is you're referring to. Why would I want to kidnap her or the child? I would prefer he disappear and I didn't have to have anything to do with him."

Zeke felt sick that he could speak of his own child in that manner. "You're disgusting."

"Maybe so, but that doesn't mean I'm involved in kidnapping and murder."

"So then you're not interested in the photos and voice mails Lisa kept from the affair. She was threatening to go public with them and ruin you."

He grimaced. "I'll admit, if I had known about them, I would have tried to convince her not to share them. I definitely would have tried to get my hands on them, but I had no idea."

"Well, someone from your office must have wanted to keep them quiet. Who else would have been as motivated to get their hands on that information?"

"If I had to guess, my campaign manager, Ethan Lloyd." Davenport frowned. "He's always been one for doing things his own way. He's passionate, but he's also brutal and competitive. He has visions of me ascending to the presidency, with him coming along. If she threatened that vision, he might have gotten violent. He's ruthless when it comes to politics."

"Where can we find him?"

Davenport motioned toward one of his security team. "Find Ethan. I need to know where he's at now." The man nodded and pulled out his phone. After a moment, he said, "He's not responding, sir."

"Keep trying. Text him that I must speak with him."

"How hands-on is this guy? Would he have abducted them himself?"

"He has connections. He has full control over a serious security team that works directly for him. That's why you so easily made it past those to protect me here. He must have taken them with him today."

"In order to kidnap Brady and Kellyanne."

The senator shrugged.

"Where would he take them?" Zeke demanded of Davenport.

"I don't know. He has a condo, but he wouldn't take them there."

The security officer turned back to him and handed him a cell phone. "Sir, I've got Ethan on the line."

Colby pulled out his phone. "I'll see about getting a trace on his line. Keep him talking as long as you can."

Zeke took the phone from Davenport and placed it on speaker mode, then mouthed, *Find out where he is.*

"Ethan, where are you?"

The voice on the other end sounded agitated. "Aren't you supposed to be at the television studio? Why are you calling me?"

"There's an emergency. Where are you?"

"On the opposite side of town. What's the problem?"

"The police are here. They think I know

something about kidnapping and murder. Ethan, what are they talking about? Did you kidnap a woman and child? Did you kill Lisa?"

Ethan was quiet for a moment, and Zeke glanced at Josh. He didn't think Ethan was going to give them a confession, but if anyone could get it from him, it was Davenport. "Lisa had damaging evidence that would have ruined you, sir. I couldn't allow her to go public with it."

Zeke saw the senator's shoulders lag, but he doubted it was for the innocent lives that had been ruined. Scandal would find him regardless, but Zeke didn't care about him, not after what he'd said about Brady. What kind of man would never want to know his son?

"What did you do, Ethan? What about the child? Where is he?"

"It's being taken care of, sir. There's no need to involve you."

"I'm already involved. You've dragged me into this. Now tell me where the woman and child are. I'm sending the police after you."

"I'm sorry, Walter. I can't do that." He ended the call, and Zeke's heart plummeted. He glanced at Colby, who shook his head. They hadn't been able to track the call. They were no closer to finding Kellyanne and Brady than they'd been before they came.

Davenport's face hardened. "He said he was on the other side of town. He owns some abandoned properties on the north end of town near the Charleston area. He's hoping to develop it and sell it to a developer at a profit."

"What kind of abandoned properties?" Colby asked.

"Houses. It used to be a subdivision, but it's all but abandoned now." He jotted down an address and shoved it at Zeke. "He could be keeping them inside one of them."

"And if he is, no one would be around to hear her cries for help."

Zeke didn't like that. He took the senator by the arm. "You're coming with us. To show us."

"I am not. I've told you what I know. I'm not going anywhere. I've got a lot of cleaning up to do here after you spilled my indiscretions all over TV."

"I'm afraid that's going to have to wait." A figure emerged from the shadows. Zeke was surprised to see Detective Shaw.

"What are you doing in Dallas?" Zeke asked him.

"I came to town to speak to Senator Davenport about the murder of Lisa Adams. I was at the police station when a report came in of several men breaking into the TV station where he was being interviewed. I should have known it would be you." He turned his focus on Davenport. "You're coming down to the precinct with me for questioning."

Zeke wanted to protest. They needed Davenport to help find Ethan, but Colby pulled at his shoulder. "He doesn't know where Ethan is," Colby assured him, "but we'll find him." He turned to Davenport one last time. "I'm certain the FBI will also have questions about your campaign's involvement in kidnapping and extortion."

Colby pressed Zeke toward the door, and he followed the brothers back outside to the SUVs. Paul, Lawson and Miles hopped into one vehicle, while Colby joined Zeke and Josh in the other.

Zeke keyed the address Davenport had given them into the GPS. "We need to hurry. Ethan knows he's been discovered. If Kelly and Brady are still alive, they might not be for long."

The brothers seemed to understand his concern. Josh started the engine, and they sped away. Zeke could do nothing but hang on and pray.

God, please keep them safe until I can get to them.

TEN

Kellyanne awoke on a hard surface. As the darkness faded, she heard crying that dragged her awake. She put her hands on the floor and discovered she was lying on cold concrete.

Where was she, and what had happened?

The crying continued, and she realized it was a baby's cry.

Brady!

She pulled herself awake and forced her eyes to open against the blinding headache that continued to push her down. What had happened to them? And how had they gotten here? More important, where was here? Then she remembered.

Ethan! He'd had one of his men knock her out.

Brady lay beside her in a blue crate. She pulled the crate closer and looked inside to check on him. He was crying and needed a dry diaper, but he seemed unharmed. She wanted to pick him up and calm him down, but getting them both out of here was her priority.

Ethan.

He was the one behind all of this. He'd killed Lisa and done his best to get rid of Kelly and Brady. She couldn't let him get away with it all.

She stumbled toward the door and tried the handle. It was locked. She pounded on it and cried out for help but heard no sounds from the other side. Either no one was close enough to hear her cries, or else they simply didn't care. She spun around and took in their surroundings. The room was windowless, so they were trapped.

She fell back against the concrete and pulled the crate to her. She touched Brady's cheek and spoke softly to him to try to get him to calm down. She wanted to pick him up and hold him, but she wasn't sure she had the strength for it. He seemed to calm as she spoke to him. He was frightened, and so was she.

She wished someone knew where she was. She didn't even know. If only she hadn't pushed Zeke away. If only she'd told him she loved him and wanted to remain in Courtland with him. But she'd been stubborn and gullible. Why did she continue to push away the people who loved her?

Tears slipped from her eyes and landed on Brady's chest. She'd ruined their chances for a life with Zeke. She glanced at Brady and realized how foolish she had been. She was a mother now, and she couldn't continue to act so irrationally.

She gasped as the realization that she thought of herself as a mother hit her. As Brady's mother.

She didn't want to lose him. She didn't want to place him somewhere else for strangers to care for him. No one else in this world would love him the way she could. If he couldn't have his real mom, she wanted to be the next best thing.

She thought about Zeke again. If only she'd come to this decision before she'd been abducted. If only she'd told him she loved him and wanted to build a life with him in Courtland.

He was a good man and would have made a good dad, and she was wrong to have kept the pregnancy and miscarriage from him. She'd focused on her own pain and sorrow and hadn't included him. She'd been afraid he would blame her, but that shouldn't have stopped her. He'd had a right to know.

Sadly, she realized now that he wouldn't have blamed her. He was a good man, and he would have been there for her during her suffering. They could have lived their grief together…if only she had allowed it.

She rocked Brady gently. She wanted so much for this little boy. More than being made to disappear or being killed by someone who saw him as a mistake.

God, please help us out of this mess before it's too late.

She might not make it out of here, but Brady had to. This child had to live.

Her eyes began to sting, and she rubbed at them. Brady coughed, and she looked down to check on him. He was burning up. In fact, the entire room was hot.

She sat up and noticed smoke seeping in beneath the door. Panic gripped her, and all her senses kicked in. The house was on fire. Had Ethan trapped them inside a burning house to get rid of them? Her heart fell at the idea that someone could be so evil.

She scooped up Brady, who began to fuss and cough. His little lungs weren't able to take the smoke. She backed away against a far wall, her eyes scanning the room for something to stuff under the door to keep the smoke at bay. There was nothing.

And what did it matter? No one knew she was here. No one was coming to rescue them.

Only the fire was coming for them.

She slid to the floor and covered Brady with her body. Tears flowed from her eyes, and she cradled him to her and started rocking. She didn't want him to be frightened.

God, I haven't always surrendered to Your will, but if I'm going to die tonight, please tell Zeke how much I loved him and wanted to be with him. Don't let him suffer.

Zeke's eyes roamed the abandoned homes, dead grass and half-downed fences. This area was deserted and had been taken over by vandals looking for easy fun. Josh rounded a corner as the GPS guided them closer to the address Davenport had given them.

Zeke's gut clenched when he spotted three men fleeing from a house and running toward a car parked at the curb. "There!" he shouted. "That's them."

He'd never seen Ethan Lloyd, but he'd looked him up on his phone as they headed this way. He wasn't difficult to pick out. The other two men were large and bulky, obvious muscle, while Ethan was decked out in a suit and tie.

Josh slammed the SUV into Park and his brothers in the second vehicle did the same. Zeke leaped out and ran toward the men before they could reach their car. Ethan saw them coming and shouted something to the other two men, who drew their weapons and started firing.

Zeke drew his own gun. "Drop your weapons," Josh called and, when they didn't, he fired, sending one of the men to the ground with a shoulder wound while the rest of the brothers returned fire.

But Zeke had his eye on Ethan. He took off running after him, catching up to him as he neared the car. "Ethan Lloyd, stop!"

He momentarily turned at his name and then spun around, pulled a gun from his pocket and aimed it at Zeke.

Zeke fired, sending the man to the ground several feet from his friends. He hurried to Ethan as he writhed on the ground. He'd only hit his shoulder, but it had been enough to make him drop the gun. Zeke grabbed his arms and pinned them behind him as Colby hurried over and slid a plastic zip tie around his wrists. Zeke noticed the others doing the same to the two men.

Zeke turned Ethan back over. "Kellyanne and Brady. Where are they?"

Ethan glared at him. "I want my lawyer," he demanded instead of answering the question. "I'm not saying anything without my lawyer." He stared at Zeke defiantly, and it seemed like he wasn't going to give him anything.

Dread filled him. If Ethan had hurt Kelly or Brady, it wouldn't matter that Zeke was a cop. Ethan would pay.

Zeke was about to query the brothers about the other men when he noticed Ethan's gaze darting toward one of the abandoned houses. Zeke followed his stare and spotted smoke funneling from the house and flames licking through the busted-out windows. His heart plummeted as he realized the truth. Kellyanne and Brady were inside that house.

He grabbed Ethan by the shirt. "Are they inside? Did you trap them inside?"

He didn't respond, but Zeke's gut told him they were.

"They're in the house," Zeke yelled, jumping to his feet.

They all turned and stared at the house now engulfed in flames.

Josh pulled out his cell phone and called 9-1-1, but Zeke knew they wouldn't get here in time. If Kellyanne and Brady were inside that house, he had to get to them. He rushed the house, Josh hollering after him.

"They're inside. I can't wait." He darted into the house. Smoke and heat assaulted him the moment he kicked open the door. It nearly sent him to his knees, and his flight instincts were telling him to get out now. But his need to find Kelly and Brady was greater.

He pulled his shirt over his mouth and pushed through the smoke and heat. He called her name but heard little besides the roar of the blaze overtaking the house. He checked the back bedrooms and found nothing. They were empty.

Panic gripped him. The smoke was growing thick, and he was having difficulty breathing himself. If Kellyanne and Brady were here, they might already have succumbed to smoke inhalation.

He headed back toward the kitchen and spotted two figures approaching him. Colby and Paul had followed him into the burning house.

"Did you find them?" Colby asked.

Zeke shook his head. "I checked the back rooms, but they're not there."

He stopped as something faint grabbed his attention. He could barely hear it over the roar of the flames, but it was there. Crying. A baby's cry.

Brady.

"Do you hear that?" He turned and did his best to follow the sound as the brothers followed him. It led him to what looked to be a laundry or storage room.

He tried the door. It was locked. He tried kicking it open, but it was firm and solid. Colby added his own strength, and the door flew open.

Kellyanne was lying unmoving on the floor, and he realized the crying was coming from a crate beside her. She'd placed her jacket over it. He pushed it off and found Brady inside.

He picked him up and handed him off to Paul, who turned and hurried out. Zeke checked Kellyanne for a pulse and relief flowed through him as he found a faint one. He nodded to Colby to let him know she was still alive, but he needed to get her out of here quickly. He lifted her under her arms and legs and carried her from the house as Colby led the way.

Josh met them as he came through the door. The sirens from the ambulance and fire trucks were still several moments away.

He placed Kellyanne on the ground and checked to see if she was breathing. She was, but barely. He turned to see Josh was doing the same for Brady. They both needed oxygen to combat the smoke that had gotten into their lungs.

The ambulance finally arrived, and two paramedics pushed him aside and started administering oxygen. He glanced over at Brady and saw another paramedic was tending to him. She'd protected Brady long enough for them to arrive to help. He was still crying, so Zeke thought he was going to be okay. She'd saved them both, because he probably wouldn't have found them without Brady's crying leading him to them.

Kellyanne still hadn't regained consciousness, and Zeke wasn't sure he took a breath of his own until she started coughing and moving. Only then did he know she was going to be okay. He fell to his knees, so grateful to God for allowing them to live.

Josh came up beside him. "You should get checked out too," he told Zeke.

"I'm fine," he insisted.

Josh knelt beside him and placed a hand on Zeke's shoulder, locking eyes with him. "Zeke, let the paramedics check you out too. Your family is going to need you."

Josh's words spoke to his heart, and he stood and walked to the ambulance where they immediately started him on oxygen. He didn't like it, but he did it because Josh was right.

His family—Kellyanne and Brady—needed him.

Noises pulled Kellyanne awake. She was in a hospital room. The smell of disinfectant stung her nose. Her throat was raw, and she pulled at the mask over her face.

"Don't pull that off, Kellyanne."

That was her mother's voice. She tried to remember why she was here. What had happened that had brought her to the hospital? Then it all came rushing back to her. Losing Brady. Confronting Ethan. Being trapped in a room in a burning abandoned house.

She jerked awake and tried to sit up. Strong

hands pushed her back. "You're okay, Kelly. You're in the hospital. Can you hear me?"

She opened her eyes and saw her parents hovering over her, their expressions full of worry. "Brady...where's Brady?"

Her mother stroked her hair. "Brady is fine, honey. He's on the pediatric ward. He's fine but they're keeping him for observation. Paul and Shelby are with him."

"Are you sure? I was so scared, Mom. I thought we were going to die."

"I know you did, but you were brave, Kelly. You took care of that little boy. You saved his life."

"I don't remember what happened." She glanced around the room and saw Josh, Miles and Colby, but no Zeke. Tears filled her eyes at the fact that he wasn't here to make certain she was okay.

"He's here, Kelly," Josh said. "He's in a room down the hall."

Suddenly fear pummeled her. "Why? What happened?"

"He ran into the house after you. He pulled you and Brady out. The doctors are just checking him over."

She sat up in bed and started pulling off

her mask and anything that connected her to the bed. "I want to see him. Take me to him."

Her mother frowned. "Honey, that's not a good idea. You need to rest."

"I want to see him now."

Fear rippled through her, and the strong desire to see Zeke overwhelmed her. Her family wanted to protect her, but she needed to see for herself that he okay.

Tears fell down her face, but Josh took her shoulders. "Kelly, I'll take you to him." He found a wheelchair and helped her into it. "You'll see. He's fine. I promise."

Her hands shook as Josh pushed her down the hall. *God, please let him be okay.* She couldn't lose him now, not when she'd gotten another chance at life. It wouldn't be right to lose him now.

"Thank you for taking me, Josh."

"Well, I didn't see any way to stop you, so I figured I might as well help."

Josh stopped in front of a door and pushed it open. Her heart pounded in her chest as the first thing she saw was Bree and Lawson standing and Zeke sitting on the edge of the bed. He was dressed and pulling on his boots. He stopped when he saw her, and his face broke into a relieved smile.

She jumped from the wheelchair, relief flooding her, and he stood and came to hold her.

"He wouldn't stay in the bed like the doctors wanted," Bree told them. "He insisted on going to make sure Kelly was okay."

"I was going crazy when I woke up and you weren't there." She stared up into his face.

He frowned at her. "Are you okay? Really?"

She smiled and leaned close, pressing her lips against his for a momentary kiss. "I am now," she whispered, then kissed him again.

He pushed his hand through her hair and cupped her cheek. "All I could think of was making certain you were safe. Nothing else mattered."

Tears flowed freely, and she didn't even care. He'd seen her at her worst.

Josh cleared his throat and motioned to Lawson and Bree. "We'll give you two some time alone."

Once the room was cleared, she pressed her forehead to his and tried to contain her tears. "I thought I'd lost you."

"I think that's the other way around." He smiled at her. "Besides, that could never happen, Kelly. No matter how many times you push me away, I'll always be here for you. If you'll let me, I'll follow you wherever you want to go. I don't ever want to be apart from you again."

Her heart soared at his statement, and she hugged him again. "There's no other place I want to be than here in Courtland with you. I love you. I want to make a life with you, but I guess I'm a package deal now. I'm Brady's mother."

"I know you are, and you're a wonderful mother. I hope one day soon you'll be a mother to his brothers and sisters too…that is, if you'll marry me, Kelly, and make a life with me?"

Tears fell from her eyes as she leaned in to kiss him. "Yes, Zeke, I will marry you. But I have one condition."

"Anything."

"That we can always stay here in Courtland and call this town our home."

His eyes held a flicker of hope. "Are you sure that's what you want?"

"It's all I want, Zeke. I love you."

"And I love you."

She kissed him again, overwhelmed by gratefulness to God she couldn't even explain. He'd brought to her a man she loved and offered her a future with a family of her own. She was done fighting.

His plans were so much better than her own.

EPILOGUE

Kellyanne stared through the window as Zeke and her brothers worked on the new barn. She was grateful they'd been willing and able to come over to help construct it. Her brothers and Zeke's friends from church had been helpful getting the new farm up and running. After seeing her commitment to Zeke and her newfound faith, Zeke's church friends had welcomed her with open arms and shown her a side to her hometown that she'd never experienced before. It was one more reason to love building her life with Zeke here in Courtland.

After Ethan and his men had been arrested for murder and kidnapping, Davenport had managed to distance himself from the scandal as much as possible. It had worked, too, and his campaign for governor was heating up.

She didn't care what happened to him, not

since he'd signed papers relinquishing his rights to Brady and allowing her and Zeke to adopt him. He was now officially theirs, and no one could take him away.

Kellyanne heard a squeal and turned to see her mother entering the kitchen with Brady in her arms.

"All changed," she stated and tickled under his chin to make him giggle again.

She was happy to see him growing and flourishing in the six months since they'd returned to Courtland. She finally had everything she'd ever wanted—Zeke, a family and a home of her own.

"Can I help you in here?" her mom asked.

"We're just about done." She picked up a bowl of salad and carried it into the dining room where she, Bree and Shelby had set the table for a family dinner. Shelby called in the men from their work, and they took a break for supper and washed up.

Zeke entered, washed up and pulled her into an embrace. "Everything okay?" he asked, motioning to her mother. She'd been nervous about having all the family here at their house, but everything had gone well so far. Her parents and the rest of her family occasionally still treated her like the baby, but it no longer angered her. There were new babies in the family now. Dylan and Brady, along with Bree and Lawson's new baby girl and Paul and Shelby's impending arrival. And, soon, she and Zeke would add a new baby of the family too.

She rubbed her flourishing belly and smiled as she sat down with her husband and family and enjoyed their first family meal in her new home.

* * * * *

If you enjoyed this Cowboy Lawmen story, don't miss the previous books in this series from Virginia Vaughan:

Texas Twin Abduction
Texas Holiday Hideout
Texas Target Standoff

Available now from
Love Inspired Suspense!

Dear Reader,

I confess, there's a lot of me in Kellyanne. Like her, I'm often impatient, hotheaded, impulsive and not always grateful enough for what God has given me. I've also dealt with guilt and shame over something that was out of my control (plus a lot of things I did have control over) and let me tell you, those negative emotions do nothing but keep you from moving forward. As Kellyanne let go of the guilt she felt at miscarrying her baby with Zeke, she opened her heart to God's healing powers and to the possibilities of love and a family of her own with Zeke and Brady. God is always the author of happy endings.

Thank you so much for joining me for Zeke and Kellyanne's story! I am having a wonderful time writing about the Avery family and can't wait to share the next book in the series with you.

I love connecting with readers. You can reach me through the publisher or connect with me through my website, www.virginia-vaughanonline.com.

Blessings!
Virginia